Double Trouble in Mystic Hills

Mysteries of Mystic Hills, Volume 2

Chris Cannon

Published by CC Publishing, 2023.

DOUBLE TROUBLE IN MYSTIC HILLS

First edition. September 18, 2023.

Copyright © 2023 Chris Cannon.

ISBN: 979-8987869857

Written by Chris Cannon.

Also by Chris Cannon

Mysteries of Mystic Hills
Murder in Mystic Hills
Double Trouble in Mystic Hills

Watch for more at https://www.chriscannonauthor.com/.

This book is dedicated to my Beta Readers: Lynn Rush, Lynn Stevens, and BB Swann for their advice and support.

CHAPTER 1

"Belinda, wake up."

"What?" I opened my eyes and saw my Familiar Sadie, in cat form, sitting on my nightstand.

"Good morning. Reed brought donuts for breakfast, and he insists you join him."

"Really?" I yawned. "Why?"

"I don't know." She lifted one marmalade colored paw and licked it. "He's all smiles this morning."

"That's odd." I threw off the navy and purple plaid comforter and climbed out of bed. "Is anyone else here?" If not, I planned to greet him in my sloth pajamas just to see the expression on his face.

"He's alone."

I brushed my teeth and pulled my chestnut brown hair into a ponytail. There. Good enough. Time for my pajama fashion show. I went downstairs and walked into the kitchen.

Reed looked up from his glazed donut and narrowed his dark brown eyes while he studied my outfit. "Are those sloths wearing berets?"

I struck a pose worthy of a runway model. "Yes. They are obviously Parisian sloths."

He shook his head and took another bite of his donut, smiling as he chewed.

"To what do I owe the honor of your presence?" I poured myself a cup of coffee, joined him at the farmhouse style table, and selected a chocolate cake donut with vanilla icing. Yum.

"I thought about what you asked me, when you first came back," he said. "I think we should start over."

I almost choked on my donut. Reed was willing to give me another chance. I never believed he'd—

"There's no reason we can't be friends," he said.

"Friends?" I asked, and then tried to cover my awkwardness with, "I'd like that."

"Good. Someone may have mentioned that I have a pessimistic view on life. They said I should try harder when it comes to people. You're the experiment in progress."

"Thanks." This may not be exactly what I wanted, but at this point I was happy to have him in my life. "I'm honored."

"You should be. Tell me what happened at the mayor's house."

"Jezelle didn't share?" I knew they sometimes dated, but maybe they weren't that close.

"She told me she fled the room because she's not good at keeping secrets."

I took a bite of donut and considered what I could tell him without violating the oath I'd taken. "The mayor is changing the restriction Aunt Teresa worked so hard to pass...the one to prevent involuntary blood donation. He's rewriting the law so non-lethal involuntary blood donations will be legal."

"That's wrong." Reed huffed out a breath. "What the heck does non-lethal mean?"

"I'm not sure. Maybe after they drain your blood until you're on the brink of death, they are obligated to call a Healer for you." It was absurd. Not that there was anything we could do about it. Witches, and the mayor especially, ran the town. He was an elected official that acted more like a king than a mayor. The witches were like noblemen. The rest of us, the gifted, the fairies, the shifters, and all the other magical creatures that made up this whacky town were second class citizens.

"Bram will have a whole new line of work as a Healer." Reed rubbed his forehead. "It's like some bad joke." He studied me. "You're holding something back."

I wanted to share the rest of the information the mayor had revealed. He'd confirmed who killed Aunt Teresa and how he'd done it. I'd love to give my friends peace of mind by explaining what happened, but the penalty was too steep. The witch in question paid for his crimes and that was the most important thing.

"Of course I am." How was he not understanding this? Frustration welled up inside of me. "I have answers to the questions we were all asking about how Aunt Teresa died, but I can't share. Unlike Jezelle, I took a vow, and I don't want to spend five days in jail without food and water."

"Five days?" His eyebrows came together. "I can't believe he threatened you with that."

I wiped icing off my fingers. "It's an effective deterrent."

"Let's play charades. I can guess what he said."

"Nope." I believed the mayor would follow through on his threat.

"Chicken," he teased.

I laughed. "Bock, bock, bock."

"What does that mean?" he asked.

"It's what a chicken says, bock, bock, bock."

"No," he argued. "A chicken goes cock-a-doodle-doo."

I shook my head. "Wrong. That's a rooster. How can you not know your farm animal sounds? What kind of preschool did you attend?"

We laughed and talked through a few more donuts. It was nice. Sharing what I could took a weight off my shoulders. Even though I wanted more, I could enjoy Reed's company as a friend.

The house phone rang. I waited for Dave, one of my housemates, to rush in and grab it. When he didn't appear, I answered. "Hello?"

"Belinda, this is Bram. Is Victor home?"

"Yes."

"Good. Reed is acting odd, and I'm hoping his father can help."

What was he talking about? "Reed's already here. He's happily eating donuts."

After a brief pause Bram said, "That's impossible. Reed is in the car with me."

I glanced at the dark haired, dark eyed man seated at my kitchen table. "Then there must be two of them," I said, sort of joking.

"I have no idea what's going on. I'm coming over. Whoever that is, don't let him leave."

"Okay. We'll be here." Had Bram been drinking? From what I knew about the Healer, he wasn't one to day drink. Was someone using a spell to impersonate Reed?

I ended the call. "Lilly, can we have bacon?" Because no one walked away from bacon.

A plate of crispy crunchy yumminess appeared on the table. The savory scent made my mouth water. I grabbed a piece. "That was Healer Bram. He wants to speak with us."

"Are you into him?" Reed helped himself to a piece of bacon.

I almost missed my chair as I sat back down at the table. "What? Why would you ask that?" Better yet, why would he care? Especially if he wasn't Reed.

"Jezelle thinks he likes you, so it could be a good thing."

"He's saved my life multiple times, so I'm fond of him." I didn't want to sound too enthusiastic in case Reed had a change of heart. Given how often he mentioned Jezelle, I was probably delusional. A tiny part of me held out hope that Reed and I might someday find our way back to each other.

The back door opened, and one of my housemates, Dave strolled in. "Good morning, my friends." He walked over to the table and grabbed a piece of bacon.

"Donut?" Reed gestured toward the box.

"Donuts satisfy human cravings. Bacon works for cats and humans."

Since he was a Familiar who took the form of a cat, this odd statement made sense. Funny to think a few weeks ago I was a normal preschool teacher on summer break instead of a gifted person who talked to the dead, accepted magic as normal, and lived in a sentient house named Lilly.

"Where's Sadie?" I asked. The Familiars were now officially a couple.

"She's sleeping in a sunbeam. I think I'll join her." He snagged another piece of bacon as he walked off.

"I should go." Reed wiped his hands on a napkin and stood.

"Bram said he'd be here in a few minutes."

I heard a car coming down the driveway. "That's probably him." I walked over to open the door while simultaneously blocking the exit. Of course Reed could pick me up and move me out of the way if he wanted, but I was banking on him going with the flow.

I glanced out the open door and did a double take. Bram strode down the sidewalk with another Reed behind him. Unlike the carefree and happy Reed standing in my kitchen, the Reed following Bram emitted waves of anger and fury as he strode toward the house. Despite my best intention to play it cool, I made a sound of surprise somewhere between a gasp and a yelp and backed away from the door.

"What's wrong?" Happy Reed came toward me.

"I'm not sure."

Bram opened the door and stepped in with Angry Reed on his heels.

Happy Reed froze, his eyes locked on Angry Reed. "Is this a joke?"

"You tell me," Angry Reed stalked toward us and pointed at his doppelganger. "Who are you?"

"Reed Clay. Who are you?"

"I'm Reed." He reached out and shoved Happy Reed.

Caught off guard, Happy Reed took a half step back but then planted his feet and leaned forward. "You want to try that again?"

The preschool teaching part of my brain wanted to tell them to take a breath and use their words. That probably wouldn't go over well. I edged away from both of them, because if things went downhill I planned to duck and cover.

"None of that." Bram's voice boomed. He pulled a glass bottle from his pocket. "Calm down or I'll knock you both out."

Everyone froze for a second.

"Belinda, what did you do?" Angry Reed turned his glare on me.

"I didn't do anything." Jerk. "Just so you know, I like Happy Reed better."

"Thank you," the more pleasant of the two said.

"Belinda, you may have hit on something. I'll perform some tests, but I think both of these men are Reed."

"What?" the Reeds yelled in unison.

Bram tilted his head like he was thinking. "I think your personality has been split into your light side and dark side."

"What?" I asked.

"Come stand by me," Happy Reed waved me toward himself. "I don't trust that guy."

"Belinda, get away from him," Angry Reed said. "Go play with blocks or something."

"Can we keep the happy one, and banish the crabby one to the void?" I asked.

Angry Reed's face turned the color of a tomato.

"Just joking," I held up my hands like I could ward off his anger.

Happy Reed grabbed my arm and pulled me behind him. "I don't think he has a sense of humor."

"Belinda, are you all right?" Sadie dashed into the room in cat form. "I sensed a threat."

"We have a situation," I said.

She glanced back and forth between the two Reeds, and then came to sit by my feet. "Positive and Negative Reeds?"

"Something like that." Bram blinked at Sadie. "You're a Familiar?"

"I'll explain later," I said. "Can you fix them?"

"I believe I can, but they'll have to work with me. Happy Reed, why don't you go into the living room while I work with Angry Reed for a moment."

"Don't call me that," Angry Reed snarled.

"How about Rabid Reed?" Sadie joked.

Reed took a menacing step toward Sadie. "Cat, I will drop kick you through the wall."

Sadie shifted into her human form and made herself as tall as Reed. "Never threaten me or mine again, young man. I've worked with generations of witches, and I will turn you into a cockroach. Do you understand?"

No one spoke. Angry Reed paled. His shoulders slouched, and he sagged against the wall. "I'm sorry, Sadie. I didn't mean that. I would never... something's wrong with me."

"Sit." Sadie pointed at the kitchen chair.

Angry Reed sat with his fists clenched. He shook his head like he was trying to shake off the anger.

"Perhaps a sedative?" Sadie turned to Bram.

"A sedative might be a good idea," Angry Reed agreed.

Bram set his medical bag on the table and pulled a small blue bottle from the side pocket. He passed it to Angry Reed. "Drink half."

He did as instructed. His neck muscles uncorded. His shoulders relaxed. "That's better. Being angry all the time is exhausting."

Sadie shrunk to her normal human size and then changed back into her cat form. "Reed, I apologize for my rude joke during your time of distress. I didn't realize how dire the situation was. Belinda, Positive Reed, come with me."

We followed Sadie into the living room. I sat on the cream colored couch and whispered, "Sadie, that was awesome."

"I may have over-reacted." Sadie hopped onto the couch next to me. "And now Bram knows about me."

Sadie's former witch had kept her a secret, letting everyone believe she was a normal cat. When I became her caretaker, she decided I was her new witch, which was kind of illegal since I was gifted. Only witches had Familiars. Hence the secrecy. Until now.

"Bram is honorable," Positive Reed said. "He'll keep your secret. On another note, am I that much of a jerk?"

"No," I said. "You can be cranky at times, but you're not aggressive."

"Cranky?" One corner of his mouth turned up. "That's a preschool term, isn't it?"

I nodded. "In class we have a cranky corner. Kids who feel overwhelmed can hug teddy bears or curl up in a bean bag chair until their cranky mood passes."

"No wonder you like being a preschool teacher." He smiled at me, and my heart fluttered.

Dave and Victor came down the staircase which led into the living room.

"What did we miss?" Victor, my other housemate, asked.

I caught them up on the morning so far.

"There are two Reeds?" Victor's eyebrows shot up.

"Surprise," Positive Reed said. "You're the father of twins."

I laughed.

Victor's eyebrows scrunched together, like he wasn't sure if we were serious. Not that I could blame him. This was an odd situation. "See for your yourself." I pointed toward the kitchen.

Victor took a few steps and then paused. "If this is a practical joke—"

"It's not," Positive Reed said.

Victor shuffled into the kitchen and then came back into the living room with a dazed expression. "I see what you mean. Any idea how this happened?"

"Not a clue," Positive Reed said. "I haven't felt this good in years."

"Belinda, can you come in here?" Bram called out.

"I don't want to," I responded.

Bram laughed. "Please. I need your help."

"Fine." I walked into the kitchen and saw Negative Reed with his head down on the table. "Is he okay?"

"He drank the rest of the potion because he was afraid he'd hurt someone. Can you find Jezelle for me? He told me she's the last person he had contact with."

I pulled out my cell phone and dialed. Jezelle answered on the second ring. "Hello?"

"It's Belinda. When did you last see Reed?"

"About an hour ago. Why?"

"This will sound weird, but there are two Reeds now."

"Is one happy and one angry?" she asked.

"Yes. How'd you know?"

"This morning, I told him he was acting like two different people."

"Any idea how this happened?"

"Meet me at *Tea & Spirits*. There's something you need to see."

CHAPTER 2

After putting on real clothes, I drove to *Tea & Spirits* hoping Jezelle could explain how Reed had been split into two people. While Positive Reed was wonderful, Negative Reed was frightening and sort of sad. Was Positive Reed the man I'd fallen in love with and forgotten? Okay it wasn't like I'd actually forgotten him. My mother had my memories removed so he was just gone from my brain.

Anyway, falling for Positive Reed...that scenario was easy to imagine. If my mom had kept her word and brought me back to Mystic Hills and restored my memory a year after I graduated college, Reed and I might still be together. Wait. That was a mental path I didn't need to go down.

At least Positive Reed wanted to be friends. Hopefully once we combined the two Reeds he'd feel the same way. Before that could happen, I needed to figure out what the heck was going on especially if this started at my tearoom.

My car bounced up and down on the cobblestones of Main Street, which seemed to be a metaphor for my new life as a gifted person who could communicate with ghosts and spirits. Before coming to Mystic Hills I didn't realize there was a difference between the two. Ghosts were recently deceased who needed help crossing over, while spirits had crossed over but enjoyed coming back to visit. Mostly I helped ghosts communicate with their loved ones before they moved on. It wasn't nearly as fun as my real job as an early childhood teacher, but I was off for the summer, so I was feeling things out in Mystic Hills.

I parked in front of *Tea & Spirits,* and then tried to go inside. The door handle didn't turn. Was it locked? As the new owner, I should have a key, but I didn't. I never thought about needing one. It was always open when I visited. I knocked. Nothing happened. I pulled out my archaic Mystic Hills flip phone and called Jezelle.

"I'm here. Let me in."

"Can't. I'm not there yet," she said. "Give me fifteen minutes."

The aroma of freshly brewed coffee drifted through the air from a nearby store. "I'm going to grab a cup of caffeine, do you want one?"

"Yes. Cream and sugar please."

A few stores down from the tearoom was a tiny coffee shop that only served regular coffee. I enjoyed fancy coffee drinks as much as the next person, but the line moved a lot faster at *Plain Jane's* than it did at other coffee houses. This morning, the line was only three people deep. I inhaled the scent of freshly roasted coffee beans and checked the area to see if anyone else was acting overly positive or negative. Everything seemed fine until the person at the front of the line became agitated.

"I said I wanted cream and sugar," a woman snapped.

"It's over there." Jane pointed to the apothecary jars that held different sweeteners and single servings of creamers. "Where it always is."

"There's no service in this place." She stalked over to the jars and grabbed a handful of sugar packets and several creamers. Her blond hair and green eyes looked familiar, but her attitude did not. Lisa Laddow was one of the most positive people I knew. A funny feeling squiggled around in my gut.

"Lisa?"

She spun around. "What?"

I took a step toward her. "Are you feeling okay?" How should I phrase this? "I have a friend who caught a magical cold that made him angry."

"I...oh my gosh." Her eyebrows went up in surprise. "I've been angry all morning. Do you think I'm sick? What jerk gave me this cold?"

"Healer Bram is at my house, if you want to go see him."

"I don't have time to see a Healer." She took her coffee and stormed off.

I called Bram and updated him on this new development.

"I had hoped this was an isolated incident," he said. "Does Jezelle have a clue?"

"She's not here yet. I'll call if she knows anything."

Once I had my two coffees, doctored with cream and sugar, I carried them back down to *Tea & Spirits*. Jezelle leaned against her blue Honda. The half-fairy's gossamer wings sparkled in the morning light. With her curvy figure, she resembled a life-sized tinker bell.

She grabbed the coffee I held out to her and downed half of it. "Thank you."

"Do you know what's going on?" I asked. "Because it might be spreading." I told her about the incident with Lisa.

"Lisa was here last night," Jezelle said. "There was a party, and...it's easier to show you." She produced a set of keys and opened the front door. Inside the combination tea room and bar the normally shiny hardwood floors featured random puddles of what I hoped was beer. Dirty glasses and dishes littered the bar top, and the tables weren't much better.

"What happened?"

"Someone brought a drinking game, and it spread through the whole bar. There were these coins with a smiling face on one side and a frowning face on the other. You flipped the coin. The smile side meant you were happy, and you won a drink. The frown face meant you were mad because you had to buy someone else a drink. It seemed harmless enough but then people started arguing or laughing really loud. Reed kicked out some guys for trying to start a fight. We let the happy people stay. They tipped great."

"I guess you would have noticed a room full of twins, especially twin Reeds."

"Yep. I'm observant that way." She sipped her coffee. "Maybe people didn't split until they woke up this morning."

"So why the mess?" I gestured at the room.

"Normally we clean as we go, but the party became wilder as the night went on. By the time we sent the last person home, I was exhausted. I purchased a cleaning spell this morning because there was no way I wanted to deal with this mess by myself." She pulled a vial of blue powder from her pocket.

"How does that work?"

"It's a ready-made spell. All I have to do is open it and say what's on the label."

The label read, *Clean and Restore so it looks like Before.*

"Anyone can use a prepackaged spell?"

"Yes. Most of them perform basic tasks. Nothing exciting, but they are oh so helpful in situations like this." She pulled the stopper from the vial and recited the phrase.

The blue powder shimmered and shot up out of the vial. It swirled through the air and worked its way around the room. Whatever it touched was instantly cleaned and the air filled with a fresh breeze scent.

"That is so cool."

"They are handy," she agreed.

A wicker basket with a leather handle magically appeared on the bar. "What's that?"

"Any stray items that don't have an assigned place go in there. Let's see if our patrons left anything interesting."

We crossed the now shiny hardwood floor and inspected the contents of the basket. There was a single gold hoop earring, vanilla flavored lip balm, a birthday card, a pack of cinnamon mints, and a coin with an odd smile face on it. I reached for it but stopped short. "Did you touch one of the coins last night?"

"Nope. We probably shouldn't touch it now."

The door to the tearoom opened, and Lisa strolled in. "Good morning my friends. Did you happen to find a gold hoop earring? When I made it home last night I was only wearing one."

I plucked the jewelry from the basket and held it up. "You're in luck."

Lisa crossed the floor and took the earring from me. "Thank you." She slipped it into her purse.

"You're in a good mood." This must be Positive Lisa.

"Why wouldn't I be? It's a beautiful day, and I had so much fun last night."

"Were you angry this morning?" I asked.

"Nothing has bothered me today," Lisa said. "Why do you ask?"

We filled her in on the Positive and Negative Reed situation.

"Is this a joke?" She laughed. "If it is, it's a pretty good one. While I appreciate your humor I have errands to run."

Should I tell her about Negative Lisa? It wasn't like she could do anything about her twin. Still if I had a doppelganger I'd want to know.

"Why do you have that look on your face, Belinda?"

How should I say this? Maybe it was best to go with the direct approach. "Reed isn't the only one with a twin. You have one too."

"What?" She backed up a step. "No. That's absurd."

"Did you play with the happy and mad coins last night?" Jezelle asked. "We think the split might be connected to the game."

"That was so much fun." Lisa rocked forward onto the balls of her feet. "People bought me so many drinks." A look of panic crossed her face. "Please tell me Nathan wasn't here."

Jezelle gave her the disappointed mom look. "Tell me you didn't give that jerk a second chance after he ghosted you."

Lisa blushed. "I flirted with someone, but I'm not sure who. I don't suppose there's a camera surveillance system in the tearoom for security reasons?"

"No." Jezelle shook her head.

"Maybe the spirits know," I said. "They hang out and watch people sometimes. Do you want me to call one of them?"

"Bad idea," Jezelle said. "The spirits gossip more than the living because it's their only form of entertainment."

"Lisa, do you feel all right?" Should I try to convince her to see Healer Bram?

"I feel great." She beamed. "Normally I have this low-level anxiety going on all of the time, but today I don't have a care in the world...except remembering who I flirted with."

"Why don't you come back to my house. Healer Bram will help sort this out."

"No." Lisa backed up a few more steps. "You can't make me." She turned and bolted out the door.

"That was..."

"Odd," Jezelle finished my sentence.

"Do you think the happy side is our more immature side?"

She ran her hand back through her hair and blew out a breath. "Maybe."

"So, we might have a bunch of happy adults running around acting like children and some negative adults acting like their angriest selves," I said. "What could possibly go wrong?"

"Should we let someone know?" Jezelle asked. "Like the police?"

"Bram knows. He's working to fix it."

"So, what do we do in the meantime?"

Good question. "We don't know how many people this affected. Can you write down a list of all the customers you remember who played the game?"

"I have a better idea," Jezelle said. "Let's go buy another spell. It will let me watch what happened here last night like a movie in my head, so I'll know exactly who was present."

"Why is there a spell for that?"

"All sorts of reasons." Jezelle shrugged. "Sometimes the elderly forget cherished memories. Other times people get drunk and need to check how bad they messed up."

I cringed. "Some things are probably better off forgotten."

"You might be right." She walked toward the door. "Let's visit Yelena and see if she can help us."

I liked Yelena. She'd helped calm my Aunt Teresa's ghost. Unlike some of the other witches in town, she wasn't power hungry and didn't feel like she had the right to take blood without asking.

When we stepped out onto the sidewalk, the mayor strode toward us like he was on a mission.

"Belinda," he said. "You're just the person I wanted to find."

"Really?" A feeling of cold dread crept up my spine. It was best to stay off the mayor's radar. He was the elected and all-powerful ruler of Mystic Hills. He was basically judge, jury and executioner if it came to that.

"I'd like you to come to the Council of Elders meeting tonight."

That didn't sound like fun, but I owed the mayor a favor since he'd shared information with me about the investigation into my aunt's death. I guess he was calling it in. "Okay. When is it and why do you want me there?"

He grinned. "I do love someone who gets right to the point. I'm going to bring up the vote to strike down the restriction your aunt created. Involuntary blood donation will be legal again as long as it's kept to a non-life-threatening level. I'd appreciate your attendance as a show of support."

"Oh." I'd known this was coming but I didn't want any part of it. My aunt had worked to ban the archaic practice of witches draining people. It was frowned upon and rarely happened, but if someone you loved was drained of blood and left for dead, no one did a dang thing about it. Blood might be the key ingredient to all magic, but that didn't justify killing people. Championing this cause had cost my aunt her life. And we'd dealt with her murderer, but that didn't change my opinion on the topic.

The mayor shook his finger at me like I was a naughty child. "I'm aware of your stance on this matter, and if I could leave the restriction in place I would, but there are too many old school families who believe the rights of witches trump the right of the gifted who benefit from all the work the witches do to keep this town running. If I don't appease them, they might not back me in the upcoming election."

Wait a minute. "This is all about your re-election?"

His eyes hardened. "This will take care of the favor you owe me. I expect you to be at the town hall by six tonight. You will smile. You will nod. You will keep your opinions to yourself. Do you understand?"

Every cell in my body objected to this plan. I had to unclench my jaw in order to speak. "If I refuse?"

"I will repossess your house and ban you from Mystic Hills for life."

And he could do it too. And he would. Which left me with one option. "I'll see you at six."

"Good girl." With that insulting comment, he turned and strode off.

Anger surged through my body like a tidal wave.

Jezelle moved around until she was in my line of sight. "You're smart enough to know that was your only choice."

Fists clenched, I opened my mouth.

She held her hand up. "Not here. I'm sure this interaction was observed."

I needed to rant where I wouldn't be overheard, so I spun on my heel and marched back to *Tea & Spirits*. Jezelle unlocked the door, and I headed straight for the bar. She took her place behind the bar and retrieved a bottle of whiskey and four shot glasses.

I grabbed the first one she filled and downed it. The burning sensation went straight to my gut. "I am...so angry. No. Furious. No that doesn't even cover it. I am enraged." In fact, I would say I was just shy of homicidal.

She drank her own shot and pushed a second one toward me.

"Guess I won't be driving." I threw back the second shot and sighed. "Why is Mystic Hills so messed up?"

"It's a town run by witches with unchecked power and populated by beings with strange magical gifts," Jezelle said. "While the majority of witches are decent, some of them are downright evil." She pushed the third shot toward me.

I pushed it back. "Not a good idea."

"Are you capable of going out in public without ranting?" she asked.

"Mostly." The alcohol had soothed my anger, but it had also stolen most of my motivation. "All I want to do right now is eat an entire loaf of French bread with butter and then take a nap."

"I can fix that." Jezelle retrieved a small clear vial full of pink powder which she sprinkled into the remaining shot of whiskey. It bubbled and fizzed. A sweet yet spicy scent filled the air.

"What did you do?"

She pushed the shot glass toward me. "Drink slowly and it will sober you up."

"Really?"

She nodded. "No one drives drunk on my watch. If anyone tries to leave under the influence, I dose them."

I had no idea magic could do that. I picked up the drink and sniffed it. It smelled familiar but I couldn't place it. I took a sip. Ginger ale. It tasted like ginger ale. By the time I finished it, my faculties were restored which reminded me, "Before the mayor dropped his emotional bomb, we were on our way to see Yelena."

"I'm ready if you are." She put the glasses in the sink and wiped down the bar.

I took a few steps toward the door and then remembered something else. "Keys. I need a set of keys for *Tea & Spirits*."

Jezelle headed over to the register and opened the cash drawer. She pulled out a purple ribbon with three keys. "These were your Aunt Teresa's spare keys for the house, her car, and the bar."

I took the keys and ran my fingers over the purple ribbon. It was Aunt Teresa's favorite color. Sadness crept into my brain. She'd only ever tried to help people in this town and look what it had gotten her. An evil witch had killed her. The idea of going to the Council of Elders meeting tonight made acid surge in my stomach, but there wasn't much I could do about it. The mayor could and would destroy my life if I refused. I put the keys in my pocket and vowed that I'd do whatever I could to change this ridiculous system or die trying like my aunt.

Entering Yelena's shop was like walking into a high-end spa. Herbs perfumed the air. Crystals hung everywhere, refracting light through the store. There was even a small fountain in the middle of the room which babbled like a brook. Everything worked together, soothing my mind and soul. The stress of my encounter with the mayor drifted away.

"I want to live here," I told Jezelle.

"I could help you redecorate Teresa's house, now that she's moved on," Yelena, a tall willowy woman with a long silver braid, said as she came into view.

"It's so peaceful here. I might take you up on that."

Yelena tilted her head toward Jezelle. "Was there something wrong with the cleaning spell?"

"No. It worked perfectly."

"We need to access Jezelle's memory of last night," I said. "To find out who was at the bar."

"Why?" Yelena asked.

"There was an issue," Jezelle said. "Someone came in with a game."

"What kind of game?"

Apparently Yelena was one of those people who required all the facts before diving into something, so I told her about the game and its effect on Reed and Lisa.

She pursed her lips and then walked behind a counter which contained amulets and bracelets. She moved a few items around and then pulled out an amulet featuring two coins set in a silver hourglass shaped pendant. The smiling face was on top, and the frowning face was on the bottom. "Is this the coin?"

I nodded.

"Then your friends played a dangerous game. This amulet allows the wearer to balance their dual natures because the coins are set. If someone wore a single coin that turned over while they wore it, or if they purposely flipped the coin over and over again, eventually their two sides would split into separate beings."

"Why?" I asked.

"The coin represents the duality of human nature. All of us are a combination of light and darkness. Based on our upbringing and societal norms we choose to behave in a positive or negative manner. Some people are in balance. Others are not."

"Where would someone find those coins in the first place?" Something that dangerous or powerful shouldn't be easy to get your hands on.

"They're not common. I've no idea why someone would use them to create a drinking game." Yelena pointed at the door. "Close and lock so I can take stock." The door closed and locked itself. "Follow me."

She led us behind the counter to a small office with an old scarred wooden table and some stools. It smelled like candle wax and dust. Candles in various shapes and sizes filled a tall narrow bookcase. Since the office was spotless, I had no idea where the dust smell came from. I was probably better off not knowing.

We sat on the seriously uncomfortable wooden stools. You'd think witches would make all their furniture comfortable. What was the use of having magic if you didn't use it to make life better?

Yelena set a round platter sized mirror in the center of the table and pulled a gray cut crystal bottle from her pocket. "We'll watch your memory here."

Jezelle frowned. "I planned to watch the memory myself. I never said I'd share."

"Do you have something to hide?" Yelena asked.

"Of course I do," Jezelle said. "It's my memory. I don't want anyone else peeking inside my head."

"Then I can't help you." Yelena put the crystal bottle back in her pocket.

"You can." Jezelle leaned towards her. "You're choosing not to. Why?"

"I want to observe how this happened. It could shed light on whether this was intentional or not."

"If you're both watching I'm not paying for the spell." Jezelle crossed her arms over her chest.

"That's what you're concerned about?" Yelena laughed.

"No, but you never give anything away for free. This will show how badly you want the information."

"Fine," Yelena snapped. "I'll pay for the spell. You will repay me by sharing the memory."

Mystic Hills maintained its weird status for another day.

Jezelle took the bottle from Yelena and downed the contents. A moment later she hiccupped, and a silver bubble popped out of her mouth. It floated down and splattered on the mirror like a soap bubble.

The bar appeared in the mirror. People entered the room. You could see their mouths moving, but there was no sound. It was like watching a television on mute. Jezelle pulled a small notepad from her pocket and wrote down the names of people as they appeared in the memory.

The women with the game came in. Their faces were blurred. "That's weird. Why can't I remember what they looked like?" Jezelle asked.

"They must have used a glamour to hide their true faces." Yelena frowned. "Those witches meant to cause chaos."

Two more women came in who were obviously related. The younger one wore a party hat that said *Birthday Girl.* "Who is that?" I pointed to them in the mirror.

"Mrs. Kingsley and her daughter Violet Fairbanks," Yelena said.

Violet's eyes were narrowed, and her lips set in a thin line. Her mother was all smiles and wild hand gestures. "The birthday girl does not look pleased."

"Not everyone wants a fuss made over their birthday," Jezelle said.

"Violet used to be as positive as her mom," Yelena said. "She's going through an ugly divorce. I'm sure her mother brought her to *Tea & Spirits* in an attempt to cheer her up."

Jezelle poured drinks for people and carried orders out to the tables. As the game spread, some people laughed and became more boisterous, slapping each other on the back. Others were pounded the table and argued, getting in each other's faces.

"Is the coin amplifying everyone's feelings?" I asked.

Yelena frowned. "I believe it could cause mood swings between the opposite selves which might explain these people's exaggerated behavior."

When Jezelle was behind the bar, Reed came over, put his arm around her shoulders, and whispered something that made her laugh. He brushed his lips across her neck right above her collar bone.

The intimacy of the gesture made my throat tighten.

The image wavered.

"Prepare yourself," Yelena said.

"I hate this part." Jezelle set the pen down and gripped the edge of the table.

The image faded and swirled, coming together into what resembled a blob of mercury, floating above the mirror. It flowed toward Jezelle, turning this way and that, lengthening and stretching out until it looked like a pencil with a very sharp point hovering in front of her right eye. It came to halt, pulsed once, and then drove into her eyeball.

Jezelle gasped and closed her eyes tight.

"That did not look fun," I said.

Yelena chuckled. "It appears worse than it is."

"No." Jezelle rubbed her eye. "It pretty much sucks because even though you know it's not a giant nail that's going to stab you in the eye, it still looks like a giant nail that's going to stab you in the eye."

I cringed. "What does it feel like?"

"It feels wet and cold and wrong." Jezelle pointed at her list of names. "Twenty-seven people came into the bar." She drew tic marks next to some of the names. "Ten random, regular citizens stayed late."

Yelena leaned toward the list and touched one name. "Nathan Gunn is the most influential gifted person on this list."

Nathan was a lawyer. "We don't know if he has split into two people."

"How many are you sure of?" Yelena asked.

"Reed Clay and Lisa Laddow."

"He runs *Tea & Spirits,* and she's president of the bank." Yelena tapped her nails on the table. "His influence is limited, but she could agree to loans she might normally decline."

"Splitting people's personalities in two might be overkill for a loan," Jezelle chimed in.

"Depends on why the borrowers wanted the loan," Yelena pointed out. "We need to find and fix the people who've split in two. If they're separated too long, they run the risk of staying that way.

"How do we put them back together?" Super glue probably wasn't going to cut it.

"Spells vary, but they must want to unite," Yelena said. "Once they agree to combine, I should be able to create a potion to bond both sides back together."

She went over to a cabinet and pulled out several small test tubes with blue liquid inside. "I'll need seventy-two hours or more to complete these spells."

"What if the people don't want to recombine?" I thought of the two Lisa's running away from us. "Will they only be half of a person?" That didn't sound good.

"Very few people are split half and half. Some may decide to ignore their other self and move on. It's a risky venture because they'll never be whole."

"Are the negative sides dangerous?" I asked.

Yelena paused, like she was weighing her words. "Both sides, unbalanced, can be cause for concern."

"We should go to the police," Jezelle said. "Let them figure out how to deal with this."

My cell rang. I pulled it from my pocket and flipped it open. No caller ID in this town meant I had no idea who was calling. Which took some getting used to. "Hello?"

"Belinda, it's Bram. Have you had any luck?"

I explained about the coin.

"I might need one to create a cure," he said.

"Yelena is working on something too, but I'll bring you the coin we have."

After I hung up, Yelena said, "I neither want nor need Bram's help." As if she was offended by the idea.

"We should go," Jezelle said, like Yelena's behavior wasn't unusual.

Weird, but I followed her lead. We left Yelena's shop and walked back to the bar. The early afternoon sun lit up the sidewalk, bringing out the crystal that had been mixed into the concrete. The scent of coffee and bread floated through the air. Despite the ideal conditions, it took effort to keep a frown off my face. The moment where Reed kissed Jezelle's neck replayed in my mind. I'd held out hope they weren't really dating, but I could no longer ignore the truth. I wanted to ask her how long they'd been together, but there was no way that wouldn't come off awkward.

When we entered the *Tea & Spirits* Jezelle said, "We need to talk."

"Okay." Let the fun times begin.

She walked behind the bar and leaned on it like she was working. "It's easier for me to talk from back here."

I waited.

"You still have feelings for Reed," she said.

"Frustration is a feeling." I tried to play it off like a joke.

She pressed her lips together, like she was trying to figure out what to say. "I know you were involved when you were younger, and then you left Mystic Hills and forgot him."

"Not on purpose." My defensiveness kicked in. My mother had given me an ultimatum. Her or Mystic Hills. She swore she'd bring me back in a year and restore my memories so I could make an informed choice. If I'd wanted to stay in Mystic Hills she'd honor my decision. But she didn't honor her word. She didn't tell me I had this whole other life. She didn't bring me back. I had no idea I'd deserted the man I'd loved.

"Intentional or not, you abandoned him and broke his heart. He'd never admit it, but I think he had total faith you'd return. When you didn't come back, he went on some benders and ended up in a few different beds."

"Was one of those beds yours?" Rude, I know, but how could I not ask?

"No." She shook her head. "I resisted temptation because I didn't want to be one of his rebounds. Over the past six months we've tip toed around a relationship. We haven't labeled it, but we spend one night a weekend together."

Bam. That information scored a direct hit like a bat to the back of my head.

"He doesn't love me." Jezelle gave a sad smile.

I sucked in a breath. "What?"

"I'm not saying he'd ever forgive you for abandoning him, but he doesn't love me."

"Then why are you with him?"

She traced the wood grain on the bar with her fingertips. "Because the fairy I loved, who I thought loved me, wanted to marry a full blooded fairy. And he did. We were together for three years. On the anniversary of our first date, I thought he was about to propose. Instead, he broke it off because our kids wouldn't be pure fairy."

What a jerk. "I'm so sorry."

She nodded. "Thanks. Reed and I are two broken people who understand each other. It's why we're good together. And you turned out to be way too nice. I wanted to hate you. But you walked in here with your pocket dresses and your happy attitude, and I realized you never would've hurt Reed on purpose."

"But I did hurt him," I said. "And before I knew he was with you, I asked if he'd give me another chance. He is not interested in going down that path again." I swiped at the tear that slid down my cheek. "Thanks for telling me. I needed to know so I could move on." But could I? I wasn't so sure. Especially with Happy Reed around.

Jezelle pulled the list of people from last night out of her pocket. She slid it into the basket that held the coin and then pushed the whole thing toward me. "Go see Bram. He's single, and he's a good guy."

Not the worst dating advice I'd ever been given. I needed to know one thing. "Did someone in his past irreparably break his heart?"

She shook her head. "No. Please don't break his. I'd hate to have to poison your whiskey."

I laughed like it was a joke, but deep down I suspected she wasn't kidding.

CHAPTER 3

On the drive home I thought about what Jezelle had shared. Reed didn't love her. She'd never said if she loved him. Loving someone who couldn't love you in return...that was tragic. Whether she did or not wasn't any of my business. They were together. End of story.

Since they were together, maybe I should pay more attention to Bram. Would he be interested in me? I had no idea. Perhaps I needed to open myself up the possibility of dating someone new.

By the time I pulled into the driveway, I'd halfway convinced myself I was fine with this messed up situation. I grabbed the basket from the passenger seat and went in the side door which led to the kitchen.

Bram sat at the farmhouse table with a mug of coffee. Funny how he seemed to belong in the kitchen, like he fit into my strange new life.

The smile he sent me was warm and genuine. He had broad shoulders, bronze skin, warm brown eyes, and wings, plus he could save my life when weird things happened, which they did on a regular basis. With Bram, what you saw seemed to be what you got. I felt myself smiling back. Maybe I should take Jezelle's advice.

"I brought you an odd gift." I held the basket from *Tea & Spirits* out to him.

"One moment. I don't want to split myself in two." He opened what looked like a tube of toothpaste, squeezed glittery silver gel onto his hands and then rubbed it in like lotion.

"What is that?"

"It's charmed to form a magical barrier between my skin and what I touch."

"It's the equivalent of magical rubber gloves?" I asked. "If I go back to teaching, I want a tube for flu season."

"Do your students make you ill?" he asked, like he'd never considered such a thing.

"Yes. As much as I love my little friends, preschoolers do not understand the concept of Kleenex. No matter how often I wash my hands or spray the room down with disinfectant, I get sick at least once a year."

"Most common illnesses aren't a problem in Mystic Hills," he said.

"So just minor magical ailments like whatever is going on with this coin?"

He chuckled, and his eyes lit up. "Sarcastic point taken. Let me see what I can discover." He reached into the basket and picked up the coin from *Tea & Spirits*, studying it in the light turning it back and forth. "I've never seen anything like it."

"Yelena had two coins set in a pendant which is meant to keep people in balance, so I don't think the coin is bad unless it's used that way."

"Like most things in life," Reed said as he came into the kitchen with an empty plate and glass. "Anything can be weaponized, that doesn't mean it's inherently bad."

I froze where I stood by table. This Reed's easy demeanor made me think he was Positive Reed. "I assume you're the happy version."

"That I am." He set his dishes in the sink. "The less than happy Reed is trying to sleep off his anger in the guest bedroom."

Was it a good idea to have him in the house? "Do you think he's dangerous?"

"I don't believe he is." Bram put the coin in a bowl and poured black powder on top of it. "He might lose his temper, but he's not a threat to the community at large. Reed, may I have some of your blood?"

"Sure." He came over and held his hand above the bowl. Bram pulled a small knife from his doctors bag and cut Reed's pointer finger. When the blood hit the powder, it swirled and turned a grayish brown. The stink of a mildewed towel drifted from the bowl.

Bram narrowed his eyes at the smelly sludge. He did not appear pleased.

"What does that mean?" Ugly sludge didn't seem like a good thing.

"It means a simple answer was too much to hope for. I have some research to do." Bram glanced away from the bowl and met my gaze. "Would you prefer I go to my house rather than taking over your kitchen?"

"You're welcome to stay here," I said. "Lilly could help set up a proper lab in one of the guest bedrooms. All you have to do is ask."

Bram shook his head. "You make me feel like I should name my house."

"You should," I said. "If your house does as much for you as Lilly does for me then she deserves a name." Seriously a house that cooked, cleaned and grocery shopped. Who would take that for granted?

"I feel my house is male," Bram said. "I'll consider what to name him."

Positive Reed laughed. "Belinda, you've started a trend."

Victor came into the kitchen. "It's nice to hear you laugh again, son. When you recombine, I hope your positive side is more prevalent."

Reed walked over and wrapped his arms around his dad. "Agreed. I can't remember the last time we hugged."

Victor appeared uncomfortable at first, but then clapped Reed on the back. "It's been too long. Want to go for a walk?"

"Sure."

I watched them head out the door and then turned to find Bram studying me.

"You care for him." The way he said it wasn't a question. More like a statement.

"I want him to be happy." It was the truth, just not the whole truth. "Everyone deserves happiness."

"Has Jezelle informed you of their relationship?"

"Yes." I walked over to fill the electric kettle for tea. I could ask Lilly to do it but I found the ritual soothing. "She also told me about her jerk ex-boyfriend who broke her heart."

"I considered poisoning him," Bram said.

I paused for a moment and then finished filling the kettle. That was the same thing Jezelle had said. Was poison a go-to for fairies? Not like I could ask, so I went with, "In your line of work that must be tempting." I turned back around, and his expression was far more serious than I'd ever seen.

"I'm not joking. What he did to Jezelle was reprehensible. All her life she's felt like a lesser being. Manuel was from one of the top families. I suspect he started dating a half-fairy as a way to rebel against his parents. If he had no intention of marrying her, he should have broken things off instead of stringing her along for years."

"There are certain people in the world I could run down with my car and feel zero remorse."

His eyebrows rose a fraction of an inch. "Ex boyfriends?"

"No. Due to my job I've encountered children who've been put through some horrific situations. I could run down their abusers without a second thought and not lose sleep over their demise." The blue light on the tea kettle flipped off indicating it was done. Time to focus on the situation at hand. "Want a cup of tea?"

"Sure."

I brewed both of us a cup of Earl Grey and inhaled the bergamot scented steam. Once they were ready, I carried his to the table.

He opened a pink cut crystal bottle and poured half the contents into the bowl with Reed's blood. The mixture turned brownish green. He huffed out a breath.

"Not a good sign?" I passed him his tea.

"I'm trying to break down the layers of magic. The more intricate the spell is, the more components are involved, and the more complicated the solution." He sipped his tea and frowned. "I don't enjoy working with Yelena, but I might need her help to figure this out."

I thought about Jezelle's interaction with Yelena and how the witch had spoken about Bram. There had definitely been some tension. "Yelena was kind enough to help Teresa when she was a ghost, but she and Jezelle butted heads today and she didn't seem interested in collaborating with you."

"Yelena is condescending to anyone in the gifted community who employs magic." Bram pursed his lips like he'd taken a bite of lemon. "She takes every opportunity to slight my work."

"So, she was nice to me because my gift doesn't infringe on her territory? Maybe your power threatens her. You're basically making potions, which the gifted aren't supposed to be able to do."

Bram tilted his head and studied me. "I always thought she doubted my abilities. Your spin on the situation makes me far less annoyed."

"Happy to help," I said.

"There's that annoying preschool optimism," Reed griped as he stalked through the kitchen and headed for the back door.

"Where are you going?" Bram asked.

"Home," Reed said. "I'd rather be angry by myself. Far less annoying than dealing with all of you people."

I pressed my lips together to keep from commenting. Negative Reed might be calmer, but I wasn't sure he'd regained his sense of humor.

"Wait." Bram reached into his medical bag and pulled out two blue bottles. "Here's more sedative in case you need it."

Reed opened his mouth like he was going to object, but then he paused and sighed. "Fine." He grabbed the small glass bottles Bram offered.

There was one other problem. "You didn't drive here." I reminded him. "Do you need a ride home?"

A sly grin crossed his face. "Pretty sure that's my car outside."

"With your anger management issues I'm not sure you should drive," Bram said.

"Whatever," Reed said. "It's only two blocks. I'll walk." He left the house through the back kitchen door.

"Are you sure that's a good idea, him being alone?" Reed might be less volatile, but he didn't seem stable.

"It's probably not. Call Jezelle and ask her to keep an eye on him."

I pulled out my flip phone and made the call. She answered on the third ring. "Hello?"

I missed caller ID. "It's Belinda. Negative Reed is walking home. Can you babysit him and make sure he doesn't get into any trouble?"

There was a moment of silence. "Where's Positive Reed?"

"Bonding with his dad."

"Okay. I'll keep a watch on this Reed."

"Thanks." Now what? I turned to Bram. "Anything I can do to help?"

He packed items into his black leather bag. "I'll go work at home in my lab. If I figure anything out, I'll call."

I opened the junk drawer which had several notebooks. "Let me copy the list of names before you go."

"None of this makes sense," Bram said. "Did Jezelle say who brought the game into *Tea & Spirits*?"

"No. Whoever it was used a glamour to hide their faces."

His eyes narrowed. "Which proves they meant to cause chaos."

"Why?" I really didn't get it.

"To distract us from something else or for the perverse joy of messing with people's lives."

"I don't care for either of those reasons."

"That's because you are a good person." Bram finished packing up his bag and then left.

Now what?

Sadie entered the kitchen in cat form and hopped up onto the table. "Any new developments?"

I filled her in on my visit with Yelena and then turned the list of names toward her.

She tapped it with her front paw. "Has anyone contacted Nathan to see if he's okay?"

Nathan and I were business acquaintances but we weren't close enough that I could call him for a chat. "Reed should call him."

The backdoor opened. Reed and his father were laughing about something. I hated to interrupt them.

"Reed, you should call Nathan," Sadie announced.

"That's an odd greeting," he replied.

"He was at the bar last night," I explained. "Can you call to see if he's split in two?"

"Sure." Reed pulled his cell phone from his pocket and flipped it open. Rather than dialing, he glanced up at me and grinned. "Any idea how I should start this conversation?"

That grin...I fought the urge to sigh and focused on answering him. "However you want."

Reed dialed and leaned back against the kitchen counter. "Nathan, some of the people who played with the coins last night are having issues. I wanted to check in and see if you're okay." Reed paused like he was listening before nodding his head. "Good to know. Call me if anything strange happens." He ended the call and shoved his phone in the back pocket of his jeans. "I think he lied to me." Reed rubbed his chin and then frowned. "He claimed he was fine, but I swear I heard two Nathan's. The one who was on the phone and one in the background yelling at him to keep his own counsel."

"Why would he lie?" I asked.

"He is a lawyer," Sadie said, "and he's used to overseeing most situations. He probably hates when things don't work the way he thinks they should." She stretched and yawned. "I'm going to take a nap. Wake me if you need anything."

I scanned the list of people who stayed late. "We should check on these people to see if they are okay. Reed, do you know Mrs. Kingsley or Violet Fairbanks well enough to call them?"

He tilted his head to the side like he was thinking about it. "Not really, but I know where we can run into Mrs. Kingsley without arousing suspicion."

"Where?"

"Some place you used to love." He walked over and put his hand on my shoulder. "Come with me. It will be fun."

I stood, and he slid his arm from my shoulder down to my hand, lacing his fingers through mine, like us holding hands was the most natural thing in the world. My brain told me this was wrong, I should not do the whole touching thing with Reed, but his hand was warm and he was smiling at me, and my heart did a happy little tap dance. "Okay."

He squeezed my hand then released it and pulled his keys from his front pocket. "I can drive."

"You almost couldn't." I told him how Negative Reed wanted to take his beloved car.

"Glad you stopped him. I'd hate for him to get a case of road rage and hurt someone or trash my car."

"In that order, right?"

"Of course. *Most* of the people in this town are more important than my car." He swung his keys around his pointer finger. "There are those few that we might be better off without."

I knew he was joking, so I laughed. I told myself I wasn't doing anything wrong. I was allowed to joke with Reed and enjoy his company. This Reed, Positive Reed, was probably the guy I'd fallen in love with. In return, he was the one who'd fallen for me. I should go with it and enjoy myself...just not too much. Because this Reed would pretty much disappear when his halves recombined. Unless...what if Positive Reed became dominant? Was that possible?

CHAPTER 4

Reed pulled into a parking spot in front of Mystic Hills Library under the shade of a giant oak tree. I tried to recall having been there before. He'd said it was one of my favorite places. Was it a place we'd visited together? While the limestone building with broad front steps was beautiful, it didn't bring up any memories. I stepped out of the car and followed Reed up the steps and through the over-sized wooden doors which looked like they could have come from a castle. The familiar vanilla scent of old books filled the air. I loved that smell, loved books, and libraries in general, but I couldn't remember any specific moments in this particular library.

A middle aged woman wearing a navy dress with a green and blue plaid cardigan beamed at us. She wore a large enamel pin shaped like a book with the word Librarian on it. She looked sort of familiar. Where did I know her from? Then it clicked, I recognized her from Jezelle's memory. She was Violet's mom. The one who'd celebrated her birthday at *Tea & Spirits*.

"It's wonderful to see you two together again," she said. "It's been a long time."

I'd let Reed field that comment.

"It's nice to see you too, Mrs. Kingsley," he said. "Belinda is back for the summer, and she wanted to renew her library card."

"Of course." She walked over to the antique oak circulation desk and logged into the computer. "Belinda, I assume you're living in your aunt's house, so the address is the same?"

"Yes."

She hit a few more keys and then glanced up at Reed. "Would you like me to reprint your card as well?"

"Sure," he said. "Mine is at home somewhere, but I'd probably have to buy a spell to find it."

I needed to ask her about the game from last night but wasn't sure how to approach the topic so I improvised. "Reed told me you celebrated your daughter's birthday at *Tea & Spirits* last night."

Mrs. Kingsley beamed. "I had to practically drag the girl out of her house. She's not been feeling herself with all this awful divorce business. In the end, she had a wonderful time. We both did."

The librarian pushed one last button on her laptop, and two gray cards shot out of a slot on the counter.

"No side effects from playing that drinking game?" I asked. "I heard a few people needed a headache potion this morning."

She chuckled. "I people watched more than I played. Seeing other people happy makes me happy." She handed us the cards. "Plus more than two glasses of wine puts me to sleep at this age. You'll understand when you're older."

Maybe she could tell us more about the game. "Sounds like everyone had a great time. I'd love to find a copy of that game. Do you remember who brought it to *Tea & Spirits* or know where I could buy one?"

"I can't remember who brought the game into the bar, but they pulled it from an Orville's Oddities bag." She leaned on the counter. "One of my favorite guilty pleasures is searching that store for hidden treasures. You never know what Orville will have in stock."

"Thanks for the cards and the shopping tip," I said. "After we pick out our books maybe we'll hit Orville's. I love a good bargain."

"You should definitely go, dear. Fair warning, I never leave empty handed. Oh, and just so you know, we've rearranged a bit since you were last here. You'll both find what you're looking for upstairs in the back right hand corner."

"How do you know?" I asked.

"It's my gift." She pointed at Reed. "He's looking for science fiction, and you're looking for paranormal adventures."

"No wonder you're the librarian." I grinned and glanced around. "The staircase is..."

"This way." Reed grabbed my hand and pulled me to the left.

Holding his hand felt so right. Part of my brain screamed that I should let go. The other part pretended nothing was wrong with this situation as Reed tugged me toward a wooden door carved to resemble a bookshelf full of books. The details were so intricate you could read the names on the spines of the books. Whoever created the door must be a Sherlock Holmes fan and also slightly obsessive because all the books were in alphabetical order.

Trying to take the high road, I released his hand and touched the intricate carving, tracing it with my fingertips. "This is amazing."

"There are all sorts of carvings in the library. Mrs. Kingsley's husband is responsible for most of them."

"He's talented." I pushed the door open and started up the stairs.

"No," Reed said as he followed behind me. "He's gifted."

"Aren't those the same thing?" I came to the landing, turned right then ascended the last six steps to a wooden door featuring a flock of birds sitting on the branches of a giant oak tree. It reminded me of the tree in the parking lot.

"Not always." Reed came up behind me and put his hand on the door. He stood so close I could feel his body heat. I stomped down on my attraction to him, and pushed through the door to the second floor, then headed for the back right hand corner. Fifteen minutes later I had a small stack of books in my arms. Reed was across the aisle searching for his own reading material.

His phone rang. I scanned a few more titles as he answered. "Hello? Hey, Jezelle. What's up?"

He sounded happy to hear from her. As he should. They were together. And my heart needed to remember that not so fun fact.

"We're at the library. Yes, with Belinda. We're following up on a lead. Mrs. Kingsley didn't experience any odd side effects. How's the more difficult me doing?"

I picked up a book with a cauldron on the cover and scanned the back. Looked promising so I added it to the stack.

Reed chuckled. "When this is all over I'll take you out to a nice dinner. Belinda and I are going to check out another lead. See you later."

I walked over and joined him. "How's Jezelle coping with the less than friendly version of you?"

"Negative me is on a fix-it mission. He can't stand the squeaking doors and misaligned drawers I've ignored for years. He's taken apart my bottom dresser drawer that sticks, and he's griping the entire time."

"You definitely owe her dinner." I snagged one more book off the shelf because I liked the cover.

"You need all five of those?" Reed teased.

"It's good to have another choice in case your first pick doesn't work out. I used to finish every book I started, but then I decided that life was too short. If I hate something the main character does or if the book veers into strange or unexpected territory I stop reading it and pick up another one." I pointed at the book he held which had a spaceship on the front cover. "You're only getting one?"

"Yep." He smiled at me. "I know what I want."

He was only talking about the book. Right?

"Let's go." He put his arm around my shoulders and led me to the stairwell.

Was he saying he wanted me, or was this version of Reed more touchy feely than the original one? It was best if I didn't get my hopes up. Not to mention I considered Jezelle a friend, so I jogged ahead of him down the stairs to get out from under his arm. If he thought my behavior was strange, he didn't say anything.

After checking out our new books, we strolled back to his car. On the drive to Orville's Oddities, he talked about things he'd like to do to his house. "The railing on my back porch has seen better days. I'd love to replace the close set spindles with something more decorative that wouldn't block the view."

"What's your view?"

"I back up to a stream and a small grove of trees. I'm sure if the mayor has his way they'll build houses out there one day, but right now I see deer and other animals."

"That sounds nice."

"We...I mean I used to love having coffee out there in the morning, and I guess I forgot about it, or I didn't notice it anymore because life got in the way. Now I can see it again."

My heart squeezed. Did Reed and I have lazy Sunday breakfasts on his back porch? If we did I couldn't remember them. It was too late now. Time to change the topic. "Are you thinking about fixing your house because your other half is in Mr. Fix It mode right now?"

"Huh." He rubbed his chin. "I'm not sure. Maybe we're connected in some way, or maybe hearing about it reminded me of things I've always wanted to do."

"It would make sense if you had some sort of mental connection to your other half. Not sure how we'd test that theory."

"I meant it when I told my dad I hadn't felt this good in years. Before I recombine with my other half, maybe we can set some boundaries or guidelines."

"People pay psychologists good money to help them overcome negative thoughts. Makes me wonder if this game could help improve someone's mental health...and maybe that's why someone created it. Although players should be made aware of the possible side effects before they flip the coin."

"Then they probably wouldn't play." Reed put on his turn signal and turned the wheel right which allowed me to see his expression better. "If someone had told me I needed to play a game because I was depressed or angry I would have flipped them off and gone about my day."

Reed pulled his Mustang into a parking spot in front of a store that looked like all the other stores on the street, except for its sign. The capital O's of Orville's Oddities swirled like oval orange whirlpools and then turned into eyeballs that blinked before reverting to whirlpools. Under the name, it read, "Where you'll find what you didn't know you needed or deserved." It could have been funny, but it gave off a creepy carnival gone wrong vibe. "I find that slogan mildly disturbing."

"Wait until you see inside." Reed unbuckled his seat belt. "Don't touch anything that looks like it might be alive," he warned, "because it probably is."

"Good to know." What kind of strange place was this?

We entered the store and...wow. Instead of aisles with shelves, a black tile path wound between circular display tables that had layers, like wedding cakes, if wedding cakes had been painted violent shades of orange and yellow. The higher the shelf, the smaller it was. The larger bottom shelves were crammed with dozens of tiny items, and the small top tiers held one large item.

The effect was unbalancing. My eyes didn't know where to look first.

A man with silver hair stood with his back to us, engaging in what looked like an unpleasant conversation with a red faced bottled blond.

"That ring wasn't hers to sell," the woman yelled.

"Lots of women sell their wedding rings during a divorce," the rail thin man replied. "I can assure you it's perfectly legal."

"Legal it may be, but that ring is a family heirloom, and I want it back." The woman stared daggers at the man.

"Given that it's for sale, you can certainly have it back, for the right price."

"I'm not paying you for my great grandmother's ring," she snapped.

"Despite your hostile behavior, I'm willing to meet you halfway. I won't put the ring up for sale right away. I'll keep it in my vault for three months which should give you time to come up with the funds. After that grace period it goes up for sale to the general public."

"You'll regret this." The woman stormed past us and exited the shop, slamming the door on her way out.

The man sighed, then turned to face us, leaning heavily on a silver tipped cane. "My apologies. Some people don't know how to have a civil conversation when they aren't given exactly what they want, when they want it."

"I work with three-year-olds," I told him. "By comparison her tantrum was not impressive."

He grinned. "Welcome to Orville's Oddities. Please wander around. I'm certain there's a treasure waiting to find you."

I was about to say we needed to ask him a few questions when a purple crystal vase sparkled at me from the middle tier of a yellow shelf. I reached for it without meaning to. When my fingers touched the smooth exterior of the vase, a wave of warmth passed over me. I smelled lilacs and felt sunshine on my bare shoulders...which made no sense since I was inside and wearing a short sleeve shirt. Still, the sensations were relaxing, even if they shouldn't be possible. Maybe it was some sort of spell the shop owner used to put patrons at ease so they'd buy more.

"It's no surprise Celia chose you," Orville said.

Cradling the vase to my chest, I turned to him. "Who's Celia?"

"You're holding her." He pointed at the vase.

I should have been concerned, but calm and warmth flowed through my body. "The vase is a she?"

"The being inhabiting the vase is a she."

I blinked out of the happy haze I'd been in. "What exactly is this vase?" The sensible part of my brain told me I should put it back on the shelf, but my emotional side hugged it to my chest and refused to part with it.

"Is she trapped?" Reed asked.

"Celia is a sprite, and the crystal vase is her home. Hold it up to the light, and you'll be able to see her."

"Reed, should I be concerned about this?" I wasn't the most knowledgeable when it came to magical creatures.

"It's an honor to be befriended by a sprite," Reed said.

I held the pale purple vase up to the light. Water or some clear liquid ran through the walls of the vase and lined the inside. Floating above the water was a tiny creature with wings. "Hello, Celia. It's nice to meet you."

Laughter shimmered through the air. A tiny creature flew out of the vase and landed on my forearm. She grew to the size of a Barbie doll with blue hair and green eyes. "Hello, Harbinger of Death. I knew your aunt well."

Technically my last name was Harbinger, and I could talk to dead people, but I didn't like to think of myself as an actual Harbinger of Death. "You can call me Belinda."

"I resided with your aunt for a time. I wouldn't mind returning to the Harbinger household if you promise to re-home me upon request."

"Of course. I'd be happy to have you as a guest." The sensation of sunshine flowed over me followed by the scent of lilacs. Celia shrank back down and dove into her vase which vibrated, then shrank and shifted until it was a purple pendant on a silver silk cord.

"Easier to travel this way," Celia's words floated up to me.

I put the cord over my head, and the pendant lay warm against my skin.

"Reed, it's your turn," Orville said.

He shoved his hands into the back pockets of his jeans. "The only thing I'm looking for today is information about a game you sold." He explained about the coins and the strange side effects going on around town.

"I don't remember selling a game recently," he said. "But so many interesting items come in and out of the store it's hard to keep track."

Gray fog engulfed me out of nowhere. Goosebumps pebbled my arms. "Celia?"

"It's not me," she announced.

The fog coalesced into the hazy outline of a woman. I recognized her from Jezelle's memory. She was the librarian's daughter. "Violet?"

"Are you kidding me?" Violet's features solidified, and she looked angry. "I can't believe that doormat killed me."

"Who killed you?" I asked.

Reed moved closer and touched my hand which, due to our symbiotic gifts, allowed him To see and hear the ghost. "Violet, what happened?"

She whooshed backwards a dozen feet. "Stay away from me, Reed. I'm not crossing over."

"No one will force you to move on," Reed said.

"We only want to help." Not that I had a clue how.

Poof. She vanished.

That could have gone better.

"Who did you see?" Orville asked.

"Violet Fairbanks," I said.

"This is turning into a peculiar day," Orville said. "Will you pay for Celia with cash, credit card, or blood?"

No matter how many times I heard people discuss it, I would never adjust to the idea that blood was used in all spells and it was also a form of currency in Mystic Hills. "Debit card. How much is it? I mean she?"

"Twenty dollars. So, you understand, it's more of a rental fee than a purchase." He took my card and walked over to a podium with an old fashioned brass cash register that had been updated to include a credit card scanner. The receipt printed, and he passed it to me over a stack of orange and yellow striped bags, which sat next to the cash register. No wonder Mrs. Kingsley recognized and remembered the bag the game came in.

"Celia, you know you're always welcome here," Orville said. "I expect to see you for tea on Sunday, per our agreement."

"Of course," Celia's voice drifted through the air, followed by the scent of fresh cut grass. "I wouldn't miss it for the world."

I glanced at Reed. He stared wide-eyed at the bottom shelf of one of the yellow tables. He reached out to touch something and then yanked his hand back.

Curious, I went to see what he was looking at. "Did you find something?"

He closed his eyes and backed up a step. "That is not something I'll need, ever again." He brushed past me and stalked out the door.

"What was that about?" I muttered.

Orville walked over, and we both studied the bottom level of the table. It held tie tacks, jewelry boxes displaying gold bracelets, diamond rings, ash trays, golf balls, cologne, and all sorts of assorted items.

That was weird. "What was he looking at?"

"I'm not sure what caught his attention," Oliver said. "Whatever it was, he'll be back for it someday."

I hurried out the door to catch up with Reed. He sat in the Mustang staring down at the steering wheel like it might hold the answers to all of life's secrets.

When I joined him in the car, he didn't glance over or acknowledge my presence in any way. Something wasn't right. "Are you okay?"

"I'm going to open *Tea & Spirits* after I drop you off. I can handle the bar since Jezelle is with the other me." He started the car.

What the heck? "Shouldn't we check on Violet first?"

He took a deep breath and blew it out. "You're right. We should. Call my dad and have him look up her address."

Life would be so much easier if Mystic Hills had normal internet. I called Victor and received the necessary information.

It took us ten minutes to find Violet's street and another five to locate her home. The stunning two story stone house sat back from the street with a circular drive made of slate. The term house didn't do it justice. It was more like a mini-mansion. "Wow."

Reed parked in the drive but didn't turn the car off. "Yeah, it's impressive. Her husband is a real estate agent. His family has deep pockets."

He adjusted the air conditioning vents. "She was afraid of me. You should probably do this alone."

He was right. I walked up to the front door, and before I could knock, Violet flung the door open. "Why are you here?"

Not the friendliest greeting. "I came to see if you were okay. I saw Negative Violet's ghost at Orville's."

"She's fine." Violet backed into the room. "Come and see."

The crazed look in her eyes convinced me I should stay right where I was on the front porch. "No offense, but I'd rather she come out here."

I heard someone struggling.

"Violet, what did you do?"

"Nothing," she said without meeting my gaze. "I mean I didn't think she was real, so I cast a spell on her. It was a little too strong. She died for a few minutes, but I revived her. It's fine. She's fine. Everything is fine."

Her manic tone told me that everything was, in fact, not fine.

"Where is she now?" I tried to peer around her as the muffled noise continued.

"She shouldn't be here." Violet said. "I don't need her. She's awful. She's the reason Herb left. Without her, I'm sure he'll come back."

Positive Violet seemed a little off kilter. What should I do? I didn't want to discuss her divorce. "Why don't you let me take the other Violet to stay with a friend? That way you can have the house to yourself."

This Violet bit her lip like she was considering my proposal and then she nodded. "You know what? That's a great idea. I need to get all the negative energy out of this house. Just one minute."

She shut the door, and I heard her talking to her other self. When the door flew open, Negative Violet stalked from the house and headed straight for Reed's car. "Get me out of here."

CHAPTER 5

I ran to catch up with Negative Violet. Once we were all in the car with the doors locked, I said, "What happened?"

She kept her eyes on the front of the house. "Drive, and I'll tell you."

Reed put the car in gear and drove. Once we were a block away, Violet spoke.

"Thank you for getting me out of there. That other me is nuts. She used a spell that put me in a coma. It was too strong, and my heart stopped for a few seconds, which is when I saw you in Orville's Oddities. She adjusted the spell and revived me when she realized what she'd done, but then she kept me tied up and gagged. Psycho."

I turned so I could see her in the back seat. "Why would she have a spell to put someone in a coma?"

"Because she's weak. She thinks she can't live without Herb. He cheated on us. I say good riddance, but she wanted to make him sick and then nurse him back to health. She thought he'd fall in love with her again if she took care of him."

"That's just wrong." I probably shouldn't have said that, but it slipped out.

"Herb and I have been together since high school." Violet sighed. "Things haven't been great between us lately, and I'm happy to move on. She can't imagine life without him or his family's money."

"It sounds like you're not split into positive and negative, more like independent and dependent."

"I think she's the old me who wants everything to stay the same, and I'm the new me who wants to start a new life. That's exactly what I plan to do."

In theory that was great. "We still don't know what will happen to people who don't recombine."

"I'll live my life, and she can live hers." She rubbed her wrists which bore faint red marks. "Thanks for getting me out of there."

"You're welcome." Now what? Should I offer to let her stay with me? I didn't know her very well, and at least one half of her was slightly unstable. "Where would you like to go?"

"I need to visit Herb at his office. We've been fighting over the house. His mother has been impossible about this whole divorce." She paused. "Actually she's been impossible our entire marriage. At this point I'm ready to sign the papers and be done with both of them."

"Shouldn't you consult your other half?" I asked.

"After what she did to me, this is karmic payback. Besides, neither of us will be able to move on until I sign those papers, so I'm doing her a favor."

I glanced at Reed. "Do you know where his office is?"

He nodded.

"I'll need you to come in with me, Belinda, so he'll believe me about the twins."

"Sure." Just what I wanted to do, get in the middle of a contentious divorce.

Fairbanks Realty was as impressive as the house. The building was made of blond stone and resembled a castle. I had no idea why a real estate office needed a turret, but it was stunning. My sandals click-clacked on the marble floor as we entered. The receptionist in the lobby did a double take when she saw us.

A side office door opened, and a tall blond who looked barely old enough to drink stepped out, and then stopped short. Her face lit up with a Cheshire cat grin as she continued moving toward us. "Hello, Violet. Are you here to admit defeat?"

"Amber, it's hilarious that you think you've won a prize. If you x-rayed Herb instead of a spine, you'd see his mother's arm. It's so far up his backside he might as well be a Muppet."

The blonde's jaw dropped. The receptionist made a sound between a snort and a chuckle.

Violet turned to the receptionist. "I've always liked you. Will you tell the cheater I'm here, and I'm ready to be rid of his sorry butt?"

"I don't think I'll use those exact words." The receptionist picked up the phone and let her boss know who was in the lobby.

Violet turned to Amber and gave her the once over. "In five years he'll probably dump you for a senior in high school."

"Maybe he will, but I'll be smart enough to have an iron-clad prenup, so he'll pay through the nose if he does."

Violet paused. "You're smarter than I thought."

Before Amber could respond, the office door on the back wall popped open. A man in an expensive suit came out wearing a cheap smile. He glanced nervously around the room. "Violet, please come in."

I followed her into his office, and we sat in gray leather chairs in front a massive desk...the type of desk a man sat behind to try and convince other people he was in charge.

Herb held his hand out to me. "Herbert Fairbanks, and you are?"

"Belinda Harbinger."

He shook my hand in a firm grip, then sat down at his desk and retrieved a file folder from one of the drawers. "Violet, I'm glad you've finally come to your senses."

She crossed her legs and gave off a relaxed vibe. "I know the house has been in your family for generations. I also know it's worth far more than you and your mother wanted to give me for it. Here's the deal. I want a fresh start in a new house which you will purchase and sign over to me."

He paused. "What house?"

"I want the house we flipped near my mom."

"The three bedroom bungalow?" He seemed surprised.

She nodded. "The one I staged with all my favorite furniture and the amazing kitchen island. The one your mother said I overspent on for the price point."

"You're serious?" He leaned toward her. "Did you plan this?"

"Subconsciously, I think I did. When I chose the paint colors and the amazing spa tub, I kept thinking this is how I'd want to live if it was just me. My own little oasis."

"Ouch," he said.

"You slept with a witch half your age who works for you," she reminded him. "And we both know your mother planned this whole scenario when she hired Amber, so be grateful I'm not asking for more."

His eyebrows came together. "Right, let's get this written up." He typed on his laptop.

"Shouldn't you have a lawyer look over the agreement before you sign it?"

Herb glanced at me. "Why are you here advising my soon to be ex-wife?"

Violet put her hand on my arm. "That's my story to tell, and I'm not ready to share yet. Print out what I've asked for, then we can both sign and be done with this mess."

He typed for a few minutes and then printed a contract which he passed over to her. "In exchange for the Fairbanks house I will give you everything you asked for, plus the provisions in the divorce settlement."

"Can we add a provision where I never have to speak to your mother again?" she asked.

He frowned. "She's not the reason our marriage didn't work."

"Please, she hated me since day one." Violet turned to me. "His mom wanted her son to marry the most powerful witch he could find."

"But you're gifted, right?" Both her parents were, so it made sense she would be gifted too.

"Yes. And therein lies the problem," Violet said. "Before his mother wormed her way into every aspect of our life, we were happy."

Herb sighed. "It's not my mother's fault. We were young and in love. I should have realized it was a fling and married someone more appropriate. Witches and gifted people aren't meant to be together. I know that now."

What. A. Jerk.

"It's like your mother brain washed you." Violet held out her hand. "Give me the papers so I can start dating a man with a spine." She read the contract, signed it, and then signed the divorce papers.

He did the same and then copied them before walking over to a wall safe where he retrieved a set of keys. "Here you go."

She took the documents and the keys and then grinned at me. "Belinda is here because some of her friends and I have been split in two."

"What?" He stared at her like she'd spoken in a foreign language.

I gave a brief summary of the double trouble.

"You're telling me this why?" he asked.

"The other Violet planned to use a spell to put you in a coma and nurse you back to health," Violet said. "If I were you, I'd avoid her."

"What?" His face turned red.

"And she's still living in the house you now own and has zero intention of leaving." She delivered this news with great satisfaction. "So good luck with that."

"Is she serious?" he asked me.

I nodded. "I wouldn't go see her alone. She's kind of scary."

"Have a nice life." Violet stood, then headed for the door with her head held high. I followed behind her.

Once we were in the car, Violet did a happy dance in the back seat. "I finally got to tell him how I felt about him, and I have my own little dream house. Can you guys drop me off?"

"Sure," Reed said.

Violet's new sunny yellow bungalow had white accents and a covered front porch. The transom above the front door featured stained glass daisies. Yellow and white daisies lined the perimeter of the house. It was adorable.

She reached between the seats and touched my shoulder. "Thanks for your help today. Maybe we could go grab a cup of coffee some time."

It was amusing that meeting for coffee was the adult version of asking someone if they wanted to be friends. "I'd like that."

I opened the car door and climbed out, pushing the seat forward. She climbed out and jogged down the sidewalk to the front door. Once she'd disappeared inside, Reed said, "I guess our work here is done."

"I think it is." I pulled out my phone and called Bram, explaining the latest development.

"Interesting. Perhaps people are split into their most opposite selves rather than positive and negative."

"Maybe. Kind of makes me wonder how I'd be split."

Without missing a beat, Bram said, "You'd be split into one half who wanted to stay in Mystic Hills and another half who wanted to go back to your normal life as a preschool teacher."

"Geez. It's like you really know me." I laughed.

"I believe I do."

I had no idea to respond to that, so I blurted out. "Do you think we need to worry about any of the other doubles trying to kill each other?"

"I hope not. You might want to check in with all the confirmed twins. Make sure they understand we're working to fix this," Bram said.

"I'll try." I ended the call and glanced at Reed. "Want to chase down some doubles with me?"

"After seeing Violet's situation, I need to talk with my own twin. We have some issues to settle."

"Okay." Pretty sure I was one of those issues.

For the rest of the drive home he stayed silent. After dropping me off, he peeled out of the driveway.

Victor opened the door. "What was that about?"

"Double trouble." My necklace vibrated. In all the fuss I'd forgotten about the sprite, Celia. "I have a new houseguest to introduce."

Victor looked around like he might have missed a person.

"Let's go inside." In the kitchen, I set my library books on the counter and said, "Lilly, we have a house guest. Celia, would you like me to make introductions?"

The necklace shimmered, and Celia flew out, growing as she landed on the kitchen table, once again to the size of a Barbie. "Hello, Walker of Death. It's nice to reside in your home once again."

Victor blinked like he was stunned, and then he smiled. "You always did have a way with words, Celia. Welcome back."

"Who is Lilly?" Celia asked.

"The house. She takes care of us, so I thought she deserved a name."

"How lovely," Celia said. "Lilly I'm happy to be back in your presence."

The kitchen lights blinked twice.

Dave and Sadie raced into the room in cat form. "I told you I smelled sprite." Dave launched himself onto the table and rubbed his face on Celia's cheek, which made her laugh.

Sadie joined Dave on the table but seemed less enthusiastic. "We haven't been properly introduced. I'm Sadie, Dave's girlfriend."

Dave paused his enthusiastic purring and glanced at Sadie. "Oh, sorry. Celia, allow me to introduce you to the light of my life, Sadie."

"You make a beautiful couple." Celia took a step towards Sadie. "I would love to rub your chin if you'd allow it."

Sadie moved forward, and Celia ran her hand over the cat's fur. Sadie immediately plopped down on the table and purred.

"See we'll all be great friends. Belinda, would you please place my domicile in your bedroom? I'd like to cuddle with the cats for now. I'll come find you later."

Victor followed me into the living room and up the stairs to my room.

"It's interesting," he said. "To humans, Celia's touch feels like sunshine. For the cats I think it's magnified. They almost seem drunk with joy."

I pulled the necklace over my head and set the amulet on my dresser where it vibrated and transformed back into the purple crystal vase. "How long did she live here with you and Aunt Teresa?"

He paused. "It's hard to say. Sprites make time flow differently. Did you learn anything about the twins?"

"Yes." I told him about the game and its effect on Violet.

"Interesting. I'm not sure what more you can do until Bram or Yelena comes up with a potion to combine the two halves."

"Something else happened." I told him about the mayor calling in the favor I owed him.

"That is..." He seemed to be struggling to find the right words and finally came out with, "most unfortunate. You can't afford to cross the mayor."

From my previous experience in Mystic Hills, I knew the mayor was basically judge and jury for the whole town. It was not a democratic system. "Any suggestions on how to deal with it?"

"Smile and nod. It's not like you can do much else. On that depressing note, I believe I'll go read in my room."

Now what? My stomach growled. Time for food, and then I'd figure out my next step.

When I walked back downstairs I spotted Celia curled up on the couch with Sadie and Dave. "I'm having lunch if anyone wants to join me."

Sadie sat up. "You seem stressed."

"Did you hear what I told Victor?" Familiars were able to hear far better than humans.

"Yes. I have no constructive advice on how to handle the situation. I could go with you if you like."

"I should go," Celia said.

The scent of lavender filled the air. I took a deep breath and felt my neck muscles relax.

"I can help calm everyone at the meeting," Celia said.

"Will the mayor allow that?" I had no idea how sprite's powers were governed.

Celia laughed. "The Mayor and his Council do not control me. I'm only bound to someone by choice. Even then that person can't make me do anything I don't want to do."

Must be nice. "Being a sprite sounds amazing."

"I enjoy it." She reached over and rubbed Sadie's ear. "Don't worry. I'll take good care of your girl."

"Thank you." Sadie flopped down, and Celia snuggled against her fur. "I believe it's time for a nap."

I headed into the kitchen and sat at the farmhouse table. "Lilly, can I have a loaf of French bread, some butter and a grilled chicken breast?" I reasoned the plain chicken breast should balance out the comforting carb-fest.

The food appeared in front of me along with a glass of sweet tea. "Thank you."

The kitchen lights blinked twice. I slathered butter on a piece of bread and took a bite. Yum. My mind went back to Herb and Violet. When I'd first come to Mystic Hills, I learned the witches were a step above gifted people, and the two groups didn't date or marry unless the witch instigated the situation. Herb probably never should have asked Violet on a date let alone married her. Especially with his controlling mother. He'd probably started dating Violet to annoy his family. Too bad there wasn't a spell to discern someone's motives before you took a chance on them.

Once I'd finished my food I decided to read until it was time to get ready for the Council meeting. Knowing Celia would accompany me made it a little less stressful. I needed to smile and nod if I wanted to keep Lilly and my citizenship in Mystic Hills. It wasn't like I had enough power to derail the mayor or the witches who wanted to drain people. Still, this whole thing felt wrong.

CHAPTER 6

Sitting in the back of the council meeting room was the only form of protest I could manage. Unfortunately, the Mayor waved me up to the front row which was about ten feet from the Council Table. He must want full credit for having me attend.

"You'll be able to hear the proceedings better from this seat." He looked at me expectantly.

Just what I wanted. "Thanks."

I reluctantly sat. If there was any way to get out of this...but there wasn't. So, I crossed my legs, leaned back in my seat, and pretended I didn't object to the mayor's plan to change my aunt's law with every fiber of my being. At least there was still a forty eight hour waiting period for hexes. That part of her legacy wouldn't be overturned. I could sit and silently fume over what the mayor planned to do, or I could observe my surroundings...see what I could learn.

There were less than twenty other people in the audience. Most appeared to be business owners. I recognized them by sight but didn't know their names. The one exception was Ann Seacourt from the jewelry store.

While I'd known this was called The Council of Elders, the Witches who filled the seats at the front table all had white or silver hair and some gave the impression of being friendly while others were visibly annoyed. The lady on the far right end of the table looked angry and slightly evil. Maybe it was the way her lips twisted in a calculated smile or the fact that she was giving the entire room the stink eye. Either way I'd do my best to steer clear of her.

The mayor banged his gavel. "Thank you all for coming to this evening's meeting. We have some interesting items on the agenda tonight."

"I see Belinda Harbinger is here," the scary woman said, "I want to hear about the events at *Tea & Spirits* last night."

Mayor Castor leaned forward. "Then you may approach her after the meeting, Agatha. That item is not on the agenda."

Agatha pointed a bony finger at me. "Don't even think about leaving without answering my questions."

My necklace vibrated and a wave of calm passed over me. Time to kill the scary witch with kindness. "I'd be happy to talk to you. Maybe we could go grab a cup of coffee across the street."

The witch next to Agatha snorted and turned her face away, like she was trying not to laugh.

"Coffee would be nice." Agatha's expression softened.

I gave her a real smile this time. Maybe she was lonely.

The mayor cleared his throat. "I'd like to start now. First item on the agenda has to do with the upcoming Summer Solstice Carnival. Every business on Main Street will sponsor some sort of family friendly game or activity. We'll pass out a bingo card with all the stores names on them. People who visit every business on the card and have each bingo square stamped will be entered to win one of several gift baskets. All in favor, say aye."

"Ayes" echoed through the room.

"We have exciting news. The high school sponsored an art contest for the juniors and seniors. The school voted and one student's sculpture won almost unanimously. Jennifer Gates, can you come forward and show everyone what you created?"

A tall slim girl with sad brown eyes stood from the audience and walked to the front of the room. She held a metal sculpture that depicted a small woman with wings, mid- flight holding sunflowers. One sunflower drooped like it was dead. The other stood tall with yellow petals that sparkled with some sort of crystals. The seeds in its center were black and shiny. "It's a sprite," the girl said. "I've seen them bring back flowers that were dead. To me they represent the bounty of the Summer Solstice."

Celia emerged from the necklace and landed on my shoulder. "What a lovely thing to say." She launched into the air and grew to the size of a barbie as she buzzed over to Jennifer. "It's beautiful."

Jennifer beamed. "Thank you."

"We planned to use a duplicating spell on the sculpture so businesses on main street, including my office, could display one during the festivities. Perhaps we'll add in a few more for our sprite friends."

Celia buzzed in a circle. "That would be wonderful."

The mayor actually smiled. "Thank you, Jennifer. If you'll return to your seat, we have several items to vote on."

Celia buzzed back to me and stood on my shoulder. The mayor ran down his list of seemingly unrelated items about the town and ingredients needed for spells. All passed without opposition.

"On to our last item," the mayor boomed. "We all know Teresa Harbinger fought to eliminate involuntary blood donation, and that was a noble goal. After consulting with multiple witches, it has been decided that involuntary blood donation will be allowed in non-lethal amounts. I cannot stress this enough. Witches may take what they need, but they may not take a life."

Anger flowed through me, but I clamped my lips shut.

The mayor gestured toward me. "Belinda Harbinger strongly disagrees with this new law, but she understands why it's needed. She is here tonight to show her support for our wonderful city that has welcomed her back with open arms."

My jaw ached from clenching it so tight. If the Mayor expected me to say anything, he was out of luck.

He called the vote, and it passed unanimously.

Celia sent waves of calm, but there was only so much she could do. "Don't forget your appointment for coffee." The slight weight on my shoulder vanished and the necklace warmed, which meant Celia had retired to her home. "Celia you're invited to have coffee if you want."

"No thank you. Agatha scares me."

"I'm sure she's not so bad." Maybe I could make a new friend. The cynical part of my brain pointed out having a friend on the Council wasn't a bad idea.

Once the proceedings were over, I wasn't sure what to do. I had no desire to talk to the mayor, so I ignored him and walked toward Agatha.

She glanced up at my approach and gave a slightly evil grin. "I thought you might run for the exits once the vote was taken."

I held my hand out. "Hello, I'm Belinda Harbinger. I don't run from a challenge. It's nice to meet you."

She took my hand in hers. "Agatha Fiend. Likewise."

"Where would you like to go for coffee? Chanda's is down the street. We could have pie with our coffee."

"Sounds good. I'd rather portal than walk if you don't mind."

Uh-oh. "I haven't learned how to portal yet. I'll meet you there."

"I could portal you," Celia's disembodied voice floated through the air.

Everyone around us paused and glanced to see who'd spoken. "Sorry if she startled you, that was my friend Celia, she's the sprite who was excited about the sculpture. She's staying with me for a while." I patted the necklace as if that might explain the situation.

"You are full of surprises," Agatha said. "However you choose to travel I'll meet you there." She waved her hand in a circle and then cut her pointer finger with her thumbnail which was oddly sharp. She flicked the drop of blood at the swirling magic and the portal opened.

"Shall I transport you to your destination?" Celia asked.

"I'd rather walk if you don't mind." Portaling still scared me, especially since I didn't know how to control the magic.

On the short walk to Chanda's, I breathed in the warm evening air. "Thanks for coming with me, Celia. Do you know anything about Agatha?"

"I know she is ancient and very powerful. Do not cross her."

Solid advice. I did have a question. "Why did she cut her finger to open the portal. Bram never does that."

"It's the old way. Bram and almost everyone under seventy has a balance of blood that they draw from."

"Balance, like at the bank? Like a magical spell or debit card for blood?"

"Yes. Portaling only takes a few drops."

I had no idea people kept blood at the bank. Unless it was a blood bank, rather than a bank that kept money and blood. At this point my brain was done trying to figure this weirdness out.

The sun had set by the time I arrived at Chanda's. The hostess led me to a table in the back courtyard where Agatha sat at one of the white wrought iron tables with a cup of coffee. I sat and the waitress joined us immediately. "What will you have?"

"Coffee and peach pie." I looked at my coffee companion. "Are you having pie?"

"Apple," she said, "with ice cream."

After the waitress left, Agatha said, "Tell me what happened at *Tea & Spirits* first, and then we can make small talk."

"Okay." I shared about the unknown witches who brought the game, described the happy and mad coins, and how people were split into twins the next morning.

"Interesting." Agatha tapped her nails on the table. "I played that game fifty years ago. The instigators set it up because they wanted someone to agree to a business deal they wouldn't normally entertain."

A tingle of excitement ran down my spine. This was my first real lead. "You were split? How did you recombine?"

"That's not important. What's important is who wanted to split those people to meet a certain goal."

Not important? I tamped down my impatience and thought about her question. "I have no idea why." I remembered what Yelena said. "Maybe someone wanted a loan they wouldn't normally be allowed to have."

"Perhaps. Look deeper into who was split and why, and you'll figure out who is to blame."

Our pie arrived, and I took a bite. It was peachy summery heaven. "Instead of figuring out the motive, I'd rather focus on how to fix the people who've been split apart."

"Your logic is faulty." Agatha pointed her spoon at me. "The only person who can reverse this game is the one who started it."

My mouth fell open. Luckily it wasn't full of pie. "You mean we have to find the witches that brought the game in and set this weird plan in motion or we can't recombine people?"

"That's exactly what I'm saying." She took a bite of her apple pie.

"I'm thinking some very bad words right now," I informed her.

"You could say them out loud. I've been around a long time. Very little offends me."

"Teaching preschool has taught me to only say bad words in my head. If I let them out on a regular basis, I might slip up in front of the kids."

Agatha tilted her head to the side like she was studying me. "Tell me about your life outside of Mystic Hills."

I shared the ups and downs of teaching preschool. "We laugh a lot, and I receive lots of unsolicited hugs. Sometimes my little people can be exhausting, but my job is never boring. When you see the light of understanding turn on in a preschooler's eyes for the first time, it's magical."

"Interesting choice of words," she said. "Do you plan on returning to the outside world?"

That was the million dollar question. I shrugged. "Honestly, I'm not sure. I don't have to make a decision for two months, so I have time to figure it out. Enough about me, tell me about your life."

"I'm one of the oldest and most feared witches in town." She gave me some serious side-eye while she waited for my reaction.

I had to swallow twice before I could speak. "Why do people fear you?"

"You really don't know who I am, do you?" She appeared amused.

"Nope."

"That's rather refreshing. Sometimes I feel like a pariah because I've specialized in vengeance hexes for seventy five years."

I gripped my fork tighter. "Why?" Okay. I probably shouldn't have said that, but it popped out.

She grinned. "It's profitable. Plus it's a family tradition."

I wasn't sure what to say. "Does it make you happy?"

Her eyebrows furrowed. This time she seemed at a loss for words. "No one has ever asked me that."

"If you've done this for seventy five years then you could probably do something else now if you wanted."

She laughed. "I'm not sure I could. I think of myself as a karma delivery service."

"Now that, I can appreciate." Wait a minute. "Did my aunt's new law which required a 48 hour waiting period on hexes hurt your business?"

"No." The corner of her mouth curved into a grin that sent chills down my spine. "The people who seek out my services are committed to their cause."

"Wow. You are kind of scary."

She laughed and we made small talk and finished our pie. By the time we were done, she no longer seemed so frightening.

After paying the bill, I said, "This was nice. We'll have to do it again some time."

"I'd like that," she said. "Remember. To figure out who set this in motion you need to see who benefits most from the people being changed in some manner."

"Most of the people who've been split apart are my friends."

"Then be doubly careful."

Once I was home, I changed into my unicorn pajamas, grabbed a notebook, and sat at the kitchen table. Who might have a motive to cause this trouble? There were too many variables.

"How'd the meeting go?" Sadie asked as she padded into the room and hopped up onto the table to join me.

I recounted my evening, ending with my coffee date.

Sadie jumped off the table, shifted into her human form, and dropped into the seat across from me. "You spent time with Agatha Fiend?"

I nodded.

"If you knew the hexes she'd created, you'd never speak to her again."

"Maybe it's better I don't know since I might spend more time with her."

Sadie shivered. "Honestly, she terrifies me."

"Well she did give me some useful information." I recounted what she'd said. "If I can figure out who benefits from these people being not quite themselves, then I'll know who did this."

Sadie tapped her fingernails on the table. "Maybe someone wants Nathan to write up a contract that isn't on the up and up, or they could want him to represent someone shifty."

"Makes sense." I scratched out a few notes. "I know Lisa has access to money. Violet was married to a realtor. Maybe someone didn't know about the impending divorce and wanted her to give them a better deal on an expensive house."

"Not to be rude," Sadie said. "Everyone is connected except for Reed."

"There would have to be some outliers," I said. "Anyone in the bar could have played the game."

"Which means there could be more twins running around town. Sadie yawned. "Tomorrow we need to confirm who was split in two.

Her yawn was contagious. "You're right. I think it's time for bed."

After going up to my room I realized there was one more person I should contact before I called it a night. I flipped my phone open and dialed Bram. It went to voicemail, so I left a message summarizing the new facts I'd gathered. Maybe he'd see something I'd missed.

I felt oddly refreshed this morning, as I sat at the kitchen table, considering how crazy life had been lately. "Lilly, can I have cranberry orange scones with orange drizzle and coffee?"

A platter of scones with butter and marmalade appeared on the table next to a plate full of bacon, a carafe of coffee, and several types of creamers.

"Lilly, I'm, pretty sure I love you."

The kitchen lights blinked twice.

Victor walked into the kitchen with his eyebrows scrunched together. "Did you tell Lilly you loved her?"

"She gave me bacon when I didn't even ask for it." I picked up a piece and bit down on the savory, crunchy goodness.

"They say a good partner predicts your needs." Victor chuckled.

A plate of blueberry pancakes appeared in front of Victor. His breath caught. He cleared his throat and looked away. "Thank you, Lilly." He wiped at his eyes and then glanced at me. "Teresa used to make blueberry pancakes every Sunday. I haven't had them since she passed."

I reached over and touched his arm. "I'm sorry."

He nodded, then picked up his fork. My enthusiasm for my food had waned. I set the scone down.

"None of that." Victor pointed at my plate. "Your Aunt Teresa would tell you life is meant to be lived. You could summon her, and she'd tell you right now."

"You're right." She wasn't really gone, I could still talk to her. "Would you like me to summon her?"

He stirred creamer into his coffee. "Not today, but soon. I want to talk to her when I'm excited about seeing her, not when I'm recovering from being sad, if that makes sense."

"It does."

"What progress have you made in your latest investigation?"

"It's funny. I never thought of myself as an investigator. Maybe it's the preschool teacher in me. I expect everything to be fair and when it's not I try to find out why and fix it."

"Not much in Mystic Hills is fair." He laughed and shook his head. "Aren't I a fabulous breakfast companion? Tell me about your notes." He pointed at my notebook.

"In the outside world in my other life I wrote on my laptop or my cell phone. Since Mystic Hills is stuck in the flip phone era, I've reverted to paper."

"The bookstore has a wonderful selection of journals if you want something more specific."

"Every teacher loves notebooks and shiny new pens." I opened my plain blue notebook and filled him in on my latest findings.

"Did anyone confirm if Nathan was split?" he asked.

"No. I could drive to his house and check on him, but I'm not sure he'd tell me the truth." I picked up a scone and took a bite. The tart cranberry and sharp orange zest made my taste buds happy. "The only other person we know about for sure is Lisa."

"How was the council meeting?" he asked.

I shared highlights from the meeting and then we made small talk for the rest of our meal. It was nice to relax and not focus on a problem for a while. Wanting the happy feeling to continue, I hid out in my room and read one of my library books. I only had a few chapters to go, and I wanted my happily ever after fix.

Sadie came into my room as I closed the book. "You look happy."

"Good book," I said, knowing she'd understand.

"Dave and I are going to have lunch up on the rooftop terrace later if you want to join us."

"Thank you. But I'm going to shower and then check on Lisa."

Once I was clean and dressed in one of my favorite maxi dresses with pockets, I called my friend.

"Hello?"

"Hi, Lisa. It's Belinda."

"What do you want? I'm busy. Make it quick."

"Are you still split in two?" I knew the answer already. Lisa was never rude.

"Yes, and the immature, lesser Lisa is driving me crazy. I can't get anything done."

"Where is she?" Hopefully she hadn't tried to kill her other half.

"She's here playing with her hair. She looks ridiculous."

"Let me talk to her. I'll see if she wants to go grab coffee."

"Just come and get her." The call ended.

Okay. I grabbed my keys and headed out to my Aunt Teresa's purple Volkswagen bug. Technically it was mine, just like the house and the tearoom, but I doubted I'd ever think of them that way.

I had Lisa's address in my phone from when she'd invited me over to her house. She lived on the same street as the Greens, who'd passed away or been murdered, depending on how you wanted to think about it. Justice had been dealt out, and I preferred not to think about that or my part in it.

When I pulled up to Lisa's house, she, or one half of her, was seated outside on the porch swing. Her long hair was a mass of crazy curls. Her hair, combined with her sweater, jeans, and cowboy boots made quite the impression. I approached with a grin. "You look amazing."

"Thank you." She wrapped a strand of hair around her finger. "It took some time, but I'm thrilled with the results."

"We are not spending thirty minutes on our hair every morning before work," the other Lisa griped from the doorway. "That's ridiculous."

"We'll see what *we* want to do once *we* recombine." Lisa stood and stretched. "Let's leave before Miss Practical harshes my happy mood."

"You better not go see Nathan," Practical Lisa hollered.

"I can do whatever I want." Lisa sauntered toward my car.

Oh boy. This was going to be an interesting afternoon.

I drove down Main Street, not sure where we should go. Hopefully she didn't really want to visit Nathan. "What would you like to do?"

Lisa continued wrapping her hair around her ring finger. "Let's go to Orville's Oddities."

"That's where this whole problem started." I told her about Mrs. Kingsley recognizing the bag from Orville's.

"Then it makes total sense to go back," Lisa said. "There might be something to counteract or enhance the spell."

"Enhance?" That didn't sound like a good idea.

"Come on." She gestured wildly with her hands as she spoke. "I'm having so much fun as anti-anxiety Lisa. The other me is stressed all the time. Why would I want to go back to that?"

"Well," I tried to come up with a good answer. "Yelena said, you'd never be whole if you didn't combine. Reed mentioned setting some ground rules with his other self before getting back together."

The car bounced up and down on the cobblestones. Lisa held onto the strap of her seatbelt. "How would that even work?"

"I have no idea." This seemed to be the theme of my life lately.

When we parked in front of Orville's, the sign had changed. The eyes now blazed yellow rather than orange. For some reason that was more disturbing. Before I could turn the car off, Lisa exited the vehicle and dashed into the store.

Was coming back here a good idea? I'd found Celia, who I deserved for some reason. Thank goodness. Did a person find something every time they went into the store? Maybe I'd keep my hands in my pockets, like Reed had. Wait a minute. I could study that table and see if I could spot what freaked him out.

When I walked into the store, Lisa was nowhere to be seen. I went over to the table that had spooked Reed. It held tie tacks, jewelry boxes displaying gold bracelets, diamond rings, ash trays, golf balls, cologne, and many other items. Could the jewelry be real? Why would a diamond engagement ring be displayed next to a golf ball? I picked up a black velvet box and studied the ring. The emerald cut diamond sparkled like it was real.

"There you are," Orville came toward me with a grin on his face. "Your friend is trying on clothes."

I set the ring back where I'd found it. "You have clothes?" I hadn't noticed them the last time I was here.

"Yes. They're in the back. This way." He turned and led me down the aisle between the yellow and orange tables. I kept my hands in my pockets, and nothing jumped out at me.

The back corner of the store resembled a bohemian boutique. Clothes hung on racks, and shoes were displayed on shelves and nothing seemed to be in any order.

Lisa popped out of a dressing room wearing an outfit worthy of a cowgirl. The black dress with a handkerchief hemline had red roses embroidered along the neckline and the hem of the skirt.

"Watch this." Lisa twirled in front of a three way mirror, and the dress flared out. "I haven't had a dress that twirled since I was a kid."

Her grin was contagious. "It's beautiful."

"I know I couldn't wear it to work." Lisa smoothed down the front of the dress. "But on the weekends this might be the new me."

"Why not?" My gaze drifted to a pair of black cowboy boots with red roses stitched on the side. "I think you need those boots."

Lisa walked over and studied them. They were much dressier than the plain black boots she wore. "I'm not sure. Would they be too much with the dress?"

"Try them on and see," Orville suggested.

"No." Lisa backed up a step. "I don't think the boots are for me."

How could she not want them? I ran my hands along the butter soft leather. "If you don't want them, then maybe I'll buy them."

"That's an awesome idea," Lisa said. "We could go line dancing."

I glanced over at Orville. "Do most people buy something every time they come into your store?"

"It varies," he said.

Nice non-answer. Another question invaded my brain. "Where does all this stuff come from?"

"Here and there and everywhere," he said, like it was a joke.

I forced myself to walk away from the boots because I didn't like being manipulated. Reed had left without buying anything, so it was possible not to be sucked into Orville's spell.

"If you're meant to have the boots, they'll find their way to you." His eyes sharpened. The kindly old man persona slipped. "I sense your distrust young lady. I enjoy connecting people with items they need. If I choose to do it in a theatrical matter for my own amusement, then that's my concern. I'd appreciate it if you didn't question my motives." He grinned and the sweet old man image slid firmly in place.

Goosebumps broke out on my skin.

CHAPTER 7

I blinked. Had that just happened? Lisa didn't seem to notice anything off about Orville's behavior. Maybe I should try to make nice. "I think you bring people joy. Mrs. Kingsley loves your store."

"The librarian? Such a dear woman. You should ask to see her cardigan collection. I've sold her a dozen, at least."

"Can I wear the dress out of the store?" Lisa asked.

"Once you pay for it, it's yours."

She followed Orville to a cash register. Five minutes later we left the store with her jeans and sweater in the orange and yellow striped bag. Lisa glided over to my car, opened the door, then tossed her clothes in the front seat. "It's a beautiful day. Let's walk to lunch."

I'd been so focused on our current problem I hadn't paid attention to my surroundings. Birds sang a cheerful tune, and the sun shone brightly. A pleasant breeze ruffled my hair, creating the perfect summer afternoon. Not too hot, and not too cold. Maybe I should work on living in this perfect Goldilocks moment where the temperature was just right.

I hit the lock button on my key fob. "It is a beautiful day. Where would you like to eat?"

"Let's go to *Chandas*. I can have a salad which totally justifies the large wedge of pie I plan to eat for dessert."

"I was there last night," I said.

"I want pie," she stated like a toddler who'd asked for candy and been denied. She blinked like she realized what she'd done. "I'm sorry let me rephrase that. Do you mind going there again today?"

"Not at all. If I ever turn down a chance to eat pie, send for a Healer."

"Oh, good. I thought you meant you didn't want to go."

As we strolled down the street, people took notice of Lisa's makeover. They smiled at her or nodded in recognition. She soaked up the attention and glowed with happiness. Had her office attire been stifling her true self? One bonus of working with preschoolers was I could wear whatever made me happy. No suit or heels required.

One woman stopped walking and gawked at her with obvious disapproval. "Lisa?"

My friend nodded at her. "Hello, Mrs. Fairbanks."

Was this Violet's mother-in-law? She looked familiar. Wait a minute. She was the woman who'd been arguing with Orville about the wedding ring.

"You won't be wearing that to the bank." She said it like a statement rather than a question.

"No." Lisa's face colored. "I have plenty of suits that meet the dress code. This is for my life outside of work."

The woman scowled. "If you're buying frivolous new clothes perhaps we need to do an audit on your department."

Lisa sucked in a breath. "I bought it at Orville's oddities, and it cost less than one of my blouses for work, not that it's any of your business how I spend my money."

"That man is a cheat and a liar," Mrs. Fairbanks declared. With that pronouncement she stalked off.

"Wow," I said.

"I know," Lisa huffed out a breath. "She really gets under my skin sometimes."

We continued on our way. When I was sure we were out of earshot, I said, "No wonder Violet left her husband. No amount of money would be worth dealing with that monster-in-law."

"Agreed." Lisa glanced back over her shoulder. "You need to be careful around her. She is on the board of directors at the bank and on practically every other board in this town. Rumor has it she's cozied up to the mayor's wife and plotting to snatch a seat on the Council of Elders once she's old enough. I'm pretty sure she hates me."

"Why?"

"I have no idea. I think she might hate everyone."

"She obviously doesn't care for Orville. So much negative energy. That would be a horrible way to live."

We entered Chanda's and approached the hostess station. Although today it was more of a host station. The handsome young man in charge of seating customers glanced at me and then he saw Lisa and whatever he'd been about to say lodged in his throat.

Lisa moved closer to the podium. "Table for two please."

"Of course." The college aged young man grabbed two menus and led us to a table near the front windows. "Is this all right?"

"Yes," she said. "Thank you."

After he was gone, I said, "He might be too young, but he's definitely interested."

Lisa tilted her head like she was considering his datability factor. "If he were five years older, I'd ask him to take me dancing."

We placed our orders, and then she scooted her chair closer to the table. "There's something I wanted to ask. Do you think Nathan was split in half?"

Uh-oh. "He claimed he wasn't, but I suspect he lied. Why do you want to know?"

She leaned in. "When we started dating, he was kind and funny and attentive."

"Nathan was funny?" He'd always seemed so uptight.

"He has his lawyer persona, but he also has a private persona that's fun."

This was hard for me to wrap my brain around. "Nathan, the stodgy uptight lawyer...that's who we're talking about?"

"Yes," Lisa said. "Which is why I want you to take me to see him. If he's split in two maybe I can talk to the fun version and find out why he ghosted me."

"He ghosts everyone," I reminded her. Nathan had a well-deserved reputation for treating women like they were interchangeable. "So, it wasn't personal."

Our food arrived. Before taking a bite of her salad Lisa said, "It felt personal. Still does. I want closure."

I understood where she was coming from, but I was concerned about her impulse control. "If you promise not to do anything extreme, we can go visit him."

After lunch I drove Lisa to Nathan's beige brick house. His lawn was perfectly green, and someone had cut it in a zigzag pattern. I parked in the street past his mailbox. "Should I wait for you?"

She grabbed my forearm. "What? No. You have to come with me."

"Why?" I figured I'd drop her off, and she could confront Nathan. Depending on how the conversation went, I could give her a ride home or she could stay and spend the day with him.

"You have to come with me. You're my cover story." Lisa squeezed my arm before letting go. "You wanted to check on him to see if he split like you checked on me. If I go by myself, he'll think I'm desperate."

"Fine." I had wanted to check in on him. Still, it was awkward for me to butt in on a possibly romantic reunion. Lisa wanted me there, so I turned the car off, and we exited the vehicle. I pressed my lips together on the walk up to the front door. What were we going to say?

Lisa knocked and then stepped to the side so it looked like I was the one who'd done it. That was sneaky. Not sure I appreciated this new character trait.

Nathan opened the door wearing jeans and a black T-shirt. I'd never seen him in anything but a suit. "Belinda?" His gaze slid from me to my sneaky friend, and a smile blossomed on his face. "Lisa, you look amazing."

She blushed. "Thank you."

I was definitely the third wheel in this situation. "I'm betting you're the Non-workaholic Nathan?"

His gaze slid back to me. "That obvious, huh?"

"Yes. You and Lisa probably have a lot to talk about, so I'll leave you to it after I ask one question."

"Okay." Nathan raised his eyebrows at me.

"You haven't tried to kill your double, have you?"

"What?" He laughed. "Why would I do that? He can work all day while I relax. This is the best relationship I've ever been in."

Lisa cleared her throat and gave him a dirty look.

"Best *platonic* relationship I've ever been in," he clarified and then held his hand out to her. "Give me a second chance, and I'll take you wherever you want to go tonight."

"I want to go dancing," Lisa said, and then waited like he might try to wiggle out of his promise.

"Then that's what we'll do."

"Wait," I said. "Don't you want to know why he ghosted you?"

Nathan shot me a look which clearly said mind your own business.

"I didn't say she shouldn't give you another chance. I'm suggesting you explain your behavior so your relationship has a chance at working."

"She's right." Lisa tucked a strand of hair behind her ear. "I need to know why you stopped calling me."

Nathan leaned against the doorframe and looked down at his shoes. "It seems petty now, but I almost missed an important meeting while I was with you. We were having such a good day I forgot to check my calendar. I pride myself on my professionalism. You distracted me. I figured it was best to eliminate the possibility of future missed appointments."

"And now?" Lisa asked.

Nathan met her gaze. "Now, I'd like to have more of a social life and be less focused on my career. No matter how this works out between us, I promise I won't ghost you again."

A smile bloomed on Lisa's face. "Then let's give this another try."

I wanted to point out the other half of Nathan may not feel the same way, but I kept that negative thought to myself.

Nathan held out his hand again. Lisa took it this time and allowed him to pull her inside. Right before he shut the door, he poked his head out and said, "Don't mess this up for us by finding a cure we don't want."

CHAPTER 8

I stood on Nathan's front porch and frowned. If people were happier this way, should we mess with them? My subconscious pointed out that if there were two Reeds, maybe I could have one of them. Nope. I should not go down that mental path. Plus it wasn't like Jezelle would volunteer to take the crabby Reed and leave me with the sweet one. I turned and walked to my car.

Without a plan, I pulled out of Nathan's driveway and headed to Main Street. Maybe Yelena could come up with something that would let the two halves live full lives. Right now she was working on a cure we might not need if we could figure out who started this whole mess.

I parked in front of her shop while I turned the issue over in my mind. Who would benefit from manipulating the doubles? What did someone want? Hopefully Yelena could help me figure this out.

When I stepped into the store, the calm vibe hit me again. I inhaled the herbal scents and smiled at the crystals in the window which cast rainbows on the walls.

"Be with you in a moment," Yelena said without glancing away from the customer she was ringing out. The silver-haired man at the counter turned to face me.

"Hello, Belinda. Did you enjoy the meeting last night?" the mayor asked.

How should I respond to his question? "I enjoyed having coffee with Agatha." There that wasn't a lie.

"Making alliances is an integral part of the political game." His shrewd blue eyes gave away nothing. "Speaking of games, I am concerned about the unusual events at your establishment the other night." His tone was accusatory.

This situation was not my fault. It wasn't like I could argue that point without sounding like a five year old, so I went with, "The game came from Orville's shop. We aren't sure who set this situation in motion. Agatha thinks

67

if we can figure out their motivation we can find the person and reverse the doubles."

"The witches who brought the game into the tearoom used a glamour spell," Yelena added to the conversation. "So they knew what they were doing. They had an agenda."

The mayor rocked forward on the balls of his feet. "That is interesting. How are the split citizens coping?"

"Not bad once they realized what happened. Most of the ones I've spoken with don't want to recombine."

"It is their business," he said. "You might want to stay out of it unless they ask for your assistance."

First he made it sound like it was my fault, and now he was telling me to butt out.

A grey fog swirled around me and suddenly the librarian was in front of me, or rather her ghost. "What's going on?" she asked.

Crap. "Mrs. Kingsley?"

"Belinda?" She peered at me in confusion. Some ghosts didn't realize what had happened to them especially if their death was sudden and unexpected.

"Am I dead?" she asked.

"Maybe. What's the last thing you remember?"

"I usually eat in the break room, but I forgot my lunch at home. I'd made a lovely batch of avocado chicken salad, so I drove home to grab it."

Yelena and the mayor watched me with wide eyes. They could only hear my side of the conversation, but they both understood what was going on.

"Violet called you earlier today. Didn't she?" I asked. "You're aware that people who played the game have been split in two. Were you split?"

"Wouldn't she know?" the mayor asked.

I shook my head and kept my attention on Mrs. Kingsley.

"I don't remember another me," she said.

"Why don't I meet you at your house," I suggested. "We can straighten this out."

"Fine." She popped out of existence.

Crud. I didn't know where she lived. "Do you have a phone book so I can look up her address?"

Yelena reached under the counter and retrieved the yellow pages. She copied the address onto a piece of paper and passed it to me.

"You shouldn't go by yourself," the mayor said.

That might be a problem. "Reed and Jezelle are busy. Bram is working on a cure. I could call Sadie."

He straightened his shoulders. "No need. I'll go with you."

I did not expect that. "Okay. I'll meet you there."

As I drove to the librarian's house, I tried to figure out the mayor's motives. Why would he want to come with me? I appreciated his concern for my safety, if that was what was going on here. He'd helped me before, but deep down I knew he was always working some sort of political angle.

At the craftsman style house, the mayor waited on the front porch, which was decorated with planters in vibrant blues and greens. All the planters were empty, which was odd. I parked and climbed out of my car as quickly as possible, then jogged to meet him. He was not a man who liked to be kept waiting.

I joined him on the porch and rang the doorbell. The ding dong echoed through the house. I thought I heard movement inside, but no one came to the door. "Mrs. Kingsley?" I called out.

"Who's there?" A woman's voice answered.

"It's Belinda Harbinger, are you all right?" I asked not sure which woman I might be speaking to.

"I'm fine. Go away."

She didn't open the door.

"Mrs. Kingsley, this is Mayor Castor. I'd appreciate a moment of your time."

The white lace curtain by the front window moved, and Mrs. Kingsley peered out. "How can I help you, Mayor?"

She obviously didn't want to let us inside.

"There's been an incident," the mayor said, "Involving the game you played last night."

"We talked about it at the library," I reminded her.

"I didn't go in to work today. I couldn't stand the idea of dealing with all those people."

This was definitely a double. "Have you seen another you in your house?" I asked. "Because people are being split in two."

"Oh dear." She ducked out of the window. I heard a lock disengage, and then the door swung wide. "I thought I'd lost my mind."

She waved us inside and pointed into the living room where another Mrs. Kingsley's lay stretched out on the couch under a cream colored Afghan like she was taking a nap.

"I panicked when my doppelganger showed up. I used a sleeping spell on her."

"How'd you get her from the kitchen into here?" I asked.

"Levitation spell." She shrugged. "I use them at the library all the time to help re-shelve the books."

"You only used one sleeping spell?" the mayor asked.

"No." She shook her head. "I used two just in case."

The ghost version popped into existence above her body. "She killed me by overdosing me with sleeping spells?"

"Not on purpose," I said.

"Who are you talking to?" Mrs. Kingsley asked.

"The ghost of your other half," I explained. "Mayor, can you counteract the sleeping spells and wake her?" He was, after all, a powerful witch.

He touched the sleeping woman's neck. His eyebrows came together. "I'm not sure if this can be reversed."

"What?" Mrs. Kingsley yelled. "I...I killed part of myself?"

"The good news is the ghost of your other half is here. Maybe if you invited her in, you could be whole again?" I said. It was worth a shot.

"Hello, other me? Sorry about the sleeping spells. You're welcome to come back."

The ghost drifted over by her other half. "I'd love to. Any idea how I do that?"

"Just dive in?" I suggested.

The ghost floated onto Mrs. Kingsley, but nothing happened. "I don't think it's working," they said in unison.

"Send for a Healer," the mayor said. "Since her other half is still alive, he might be able to revive her."

"I'll call Bram." I trusted him.

"That's settled," the mayor said. "Belinda keep me apprised of any new discoveries regarding the witches responsible for this." With those words he left.

I called Bram, and he portaled into Mrs. Kingsley's living room five minutes later. After examining the body on the couch, he said, "I'm not sure if this will work. Since half of her spirit is still alive, I hope to revive her." He pulled out his bowl and crystal bottles, then took blood from the awake Mrs. Kingsley.

He created a green mixture which smelled of limes and shifted the hopefully sleeping body to a seated position. He gave her droppers full of the potion. After a tense ten minutes, the ghost began to shimmer and then she poofed out of existence as the sleeping woman's eyes opened.

"Thank goodness," the other Mrs. Kingsley said. "I'm so sorry."

The previously ghostly woman said, "Can we recombine and be done with this, please?"

"I'd like that." They reached for each other's hands and then hugged. Nothing happened.

"Why aren't we together?" they asked in unison.

"I have no idea." Frustration bled through Bram's voice. "This may be beyond my gift. I create potions to heal ailments and injuries. Perhaps when you're split you aren't considered injured."

"Either way you saved my life," one half of Mrs. Kingsley said. "So, thank you, and don't be so hard on yourself."

"I have a large batch of avocado chicken salad if you haven't had lunch yet," the other Mrs. Kingsley offered.

"No thank you," Bram said. "I've already eaten."

"Me too," I said. "We'll leave you to your lunch. Bram, I drove here if you want a ride."

"I'd like that." We headed out the front door to my car.

"Did you get my message from last night?" I asked him.

"Yes. I can't believe you spent time with Agatha Fiend. Her hexes are the stuff of nightmares."

"I'd rather not know about them. I think she gave me good advice. She's been through this before. We need to figure out who did this so they can fix it."

"Maybe it's time to go back to where this all started?" Bram said as he climbed into my car.

"Orville's Oddities?" I turned the key, and the engine roared to life.

"No. Maybe you missed something at *Tea & Spirits.*"

I wasn't sure what we could find there. "Okay. If we don't find any clues there, we can go talk to Yelena."

He sighed. "I'll need a drink before I deal with that woman."

"Then it's a good thing that *Tea & Spirits* bar is fully stocked."

CHAPTER 9

When we arrived at *Tea & Spirits*, I was surprised me to see it open. "Huh. Reed and Jezelle must have decided to come in to work."

"Keeping busy is often the best way to take your mind off of your troubles," Bram said as we climbed out of the car.

He held the door to the tearoom open for me.

"Thank you."

It wasn't like Jezelle and Reed needed my permission to open. These were normal business hours. I just thought the tearoom would be closed given the extenuating circumstances.

Half the tables were full of people drinking and talking. Some were playing cards. Two Reeds stood behind the bar chatting with Jezelle. "I thought they'd lay low."

"All three of them look happy, or at least content," Bram said as we headed toward the bar.

I wasn't sure what to make of this situation. Jezelle greeted me with a cup of peppermint tea and handed Bram a mug full of dark ale. Her gift was that she knew exactly what drink someone needed, even if they didn't know themselves. And yes, her gift was way better than mine.

Bram glanced at the mug and then back at Jezelle. "Interesting choice."

"For courage," she said. "I'm not sure why you need it."

"We're considering visiting Yelena to see if she's figured out how to recombine people." I sipped my tea and realized everyone was staring at me. "What?"

"We're waiting for the lecture," one of the Reeds said.

"What lecture?" I had no idea what he was talking about.

"The one where you tell us we should be laying low," the other Reed said. "Trying to protect people is in your preschool teaching DNA."

"True, but you're all adults capable of making your own choices." No way would I tell them I'd used those exact same words when I entered the bar. Hopefully Bram wouldn't rat me out.

Jezelle grabbed the tip jar and held it toward them. "Pay up."

Both Reeds slapped ten dollar bills into the jar. "I said you wouldn't lecture them." She smiled. "Guess I know you better than they do."

"Speaking of them." I pointed at the two Reeds. "How'd you—?" I wasn't sure how to say what I meant. "Balance them out?"

"She didn't do this," the closer Reed said. "We had a heart to heart, and talked through some issues."

"It's not like we had a freaking Hallmark moment," the other Reed griped.

"At least now I know who is who." I wanted to get back at them in some manner. "I dub thee Cranky Reed and Non-cranky Reed."

Jezelle laughed. "I refer to them as Happy and Grumpy, like the dwarves from Snow White.

"I'm glad to see you're all doing well." Bram placed his hand on my arm. "Why don't we brainstorm in your office. See if we can figure this out."

His touch was warm and comforting.

"You don't want to brainstorm with us?" Jezelle said, like she was offended.

"You're welcome to join us. It's not something we should discuss out here." Bram waved his hand, indicating the other patrons. "We still don't know who is behind this."

"You two have fun," Jezelle said. "We've hashed over this issue a dozen times and haven't been able to figure out why someone would want a bunch of twins running around Mystic Hills."

"Let's use Reed's office," I said. "Mine is like a closet."

"You own the bar, so you can probably pick your office," Bram said.

"No, she can't," both Reeds said at the same time.

I laughed. "We'll see about that." I led Bram over to what had been my Aunt Teresa's office, which Reed had taken over. I sat in the black leather chair, and Bram leaned against the antique desk. He opened his mouth to speak and then stood and walked behind the desk, picked up the chair and carried it around so he was seated in front of me.

"That's better. I've never liked talking to someone who stood while I sat. Reminds me too much of being in trouble at school."

"You were a troublemaker? That's hard to imagine."

"Not to sound arrogant, but I understood things faster than most of my classmates. I've always enjoyed helping others, so I would explain assignments to my friends, and sometimes, according to my teachers, I over-helped."

"It's strange that you'd get into trouble for helping."

"From an adult perspective I understand how me re-teaching the lessons could have annoyed the teachers." He set his drink on his knee. "I've come up with a mental list of why someone would want to increase the number of citizens in Mystic Hills. Do you want to hear it?"

"Yes." I sipped my tea and waited.

"Okay, here we go." He counted items off on his fingers. "It might be a way to secure more votes. If both halves are allowed to vote. Also, both halves would be required to pay taxes."

Wait a minute. "Taxes are paid in blood. Do you think this is about blood?"

"In Mystic Hills blood is power," Bram said.

"Agatha suggested that whoever put this in motion did it to coerce someone else into giving them something they wanted. They may have only meant to split one individual."

"That would make the other twins collateral damage." Bram sipped his ale. "So, who was the real target?"

"It's not like Reed can do much for anyone," I said, thinking out loud.

"Excuse me?" Reed strolled into the room. The smile on his face told me it was Non-Cranky Reed.

"We're trying to figure out who could be used for some sort of financial gain or a power grab. "You, Violet, and the librarian aren't high profile people."

"True. So someone is trying to manipulate a lawyer or a banker?"

"That would make the most sense," I said.

A gray form swirled and came to stop in front of me. "Violet?"

"What did you do?" She yelled at me.

I jerked backwards in my seat, sloshing my tea in the cup. "What happened?" I asked. "Where are you?"

"Drained." Her image went fuzzy.

"Violet, who drained you?"

She snapped and crackled, then disappeared.

"Which Violet was it?" Bram asked.

"I think it was the one who wanted Herb back."

Bram grabbed his phone and dialed the police. "I'd like to report the possible death of Violet Fairbanks. She might be at her house." He paused listening. "Yes. Of course. We'll meet you there." He ended the call.

"I'll drive," Non-cranky Reed said.

After a quick explanation to Jezelle and Cranky Reed, we took off.

Before we left Main Street, an idea hit me. "We should check Independent Violet's house to make sure it's not her before we go to the Fairbanks house." I could be wrong. I hoped I wasn't. That made me feel like a bad person, because neither Violet deserved to die.

When we reached Independent Violet's new yellow bungalow, I knocked on the front door. No one answered. I knocked again.

Violet answered. "Hey Belinda.... wait what's wrong?"

"I think someone drained your other half. You need to be careful."

"Oh." Violet placed her hand on the doorframe as if to steady herself. "That's not good." She glanced around. "Very few people know about this house, so I should be safe."

"Have you talked to your mom?"

"Yes." Violet nodded. "Both of them. They're coming over for dinner."

"Good. You should keep an eye on each other in case someone is draining twins."

"That's a horrifying thought." Violet crossed her arms over her chest. "I'll call my father and ask him to come home early, too."

"Good idea," I said.

"Let me know what you discover," Violet said. "And watch your back. I wouldn't put it beyond the other me to set up some sort of trap."

Great. I hadn't thought of that.

When I climbed back into the Mustang, I shared Violet's message.

"She was kind of crazy," Non-cranky Reed said. "I don't think anyone would fake death by drainage."

When we showed up at the Fairbanks house, the police were already there.

"Why don't you let me go first," Bram said.

Non-cranky Reed and I stayed in the car while Bram approached the police. After a short conversation he waved at us to join him.

"Did you find her?" I asked.

The police officer nodded. "Drained, in the kitchen. There wasn't any sign of a struggle."

"So, she knew the person who killed her?" I guessed.

"We're working on that assumption," the officer said. "There were two cups of coffee on the table. Could have been from breakfast but I doubt it." He pointed at me. "You're the ghost whisperer. Can you talk to her? See what she knows?"

I cleared my throat. "I can try. Violet Fairbanks, please come speak to me."

Her ghost materialized next to the officer.

"Who did this?" I asked.

"Who?" Her form swirled.

"Yes. Who drained you?"

"It was her." Violet snapped.

"Who?"

"Mother-in-law."

Oh crap. If what Lisa had told me was true, Mrs. Fairbanks was a powerful witch in this town. I needed to phrase this carefully. "The last thing she remembers is talking to her mother in law."

The officer took a step back. "Mrs. Fairbanks? Are you accusing her of something?"

"No. I'm saying she was the last person Violet saw or spoke to when she was alive."

"We aren't accusing Mrs. Fairbanks of anything," Reed assured him. "Maybe she could shed some light on how this happened."

"Mrs. Fairbanks is highly regarded," the officer said. "She is always above suspicion. Always." He moved closer like he was trying to convey a message. "In my history on the force, not a single complaint against a Fairbanks has been investigated. Not one."

So even if a complaint was filed against a Fairbanks, it was never investigated which meant they never suffered any consequences for their actions. Wonderful. Time to practice my diplomacy skills. "Mrs. Fairbanks probably visited her daughter-in-law to discuss the divorce settlement which was signed earlier today." And maybe she'd decided her son didn't need to buy his ex-wife a new house. Being widowed would be far more convenient not to mention cheaper.

"That was probably it." The officer nodded. "Since we aren't sure, I won't mention it in my report." He walked to his police cruiser and leaned back against it while he used his flip phone to make a call.

Violet swirled and appeared a foot in front of my face. "I'm still here."

"We'll help you," I whispered. "This is pretend. You won't really cross over. Play along." At a normal volume, I said, "Reed you're up."

Reed grabbed my hand so he could see and hear Violet through our symbiotic connection. This was how we fit together. I could always see and hear the ghosts. He couldn't do either unless we had some sort of skin contact. Warmth crept up my arm to my heart. My brain reminded me that Reed and I weren't together. My heart refused to believe.

"You won't force me to pass over." Violet sounded desperate.

My heart ached for her.

"I won't." Reed closed his eyes and started to glow but it was weak compared to the radiance of the sun he normally displayed when he crossed people over. When he opened his eyes, he appeared calm.

Violet's ghost went all staticky. She screamed and then disappeared. Hopefully she understood we were trying to help.

"Now what?" Reed asked.

"We still have a puzzle to solve," Bram said.

"Maybe we could talk to the people who've been through this before. I could call Agatha and see if she remembers any more details."

Bram shot me a look of frustration. Once we were in the car driving back to *Tea & Spirits* he said, "Belinda, I don't think you understand what Agatha does."

"She creates vengeance hexes for seriously angry people."

Bram frowned. "It's more than that. She creates what she believes is karmic justice. And her versions of justice are...I don't even know how to describe them."

What was his problem? "I'm not saying I want to have a slumber party with her and braid her hair. I think she might have useful information."

"For a price," Reed said. "Nothing in this town is free. Did you forget that?"

My head started to pound. "No. She shared information with me because she wanted to know what happened."

"Did you tell her who was split?" Reed asked.

Had I? "I don't think so."

Once we reached the teahouse we reconvened in Reed's office. Jezelle and the other Reed joined us.

"Before we get started, I need you to understand something," Bram's tone was more serious than usual. "Agatha was hired to create a vengeance hex for a woman whose husband slept around and impregnated two other witches. She must have referred to her husband as a snake, and rightfully so. Agatha crafted a hex that caused him to shed his skin. As his skin continued to come off in layers there was nothing I could do to help him except ease some of his pain. He lost his nose, his ears, and other dangling appendages."

Both Reeds sucked in a breath.

A wave of nausea hit me. "You don't mean—"

"Yes," Bram said. "She castrated him. Slowly. One layer of skin at a time."

I couldn't comprehend it. "That is...it's—"

"Pure evil," Bram stated. "No one deserves what that man went through."

"Did it eventually kill him?" Jezelle asked.

Bram shook his head. "He might have been better off. Once he stopped shedding, his wife explained why she'd hexed him. She asked Agatha to remove the hex, which she did. The man's body healed slowly over weeks but mentally he never recovered. A few days after his body was whole, he took his own life."

My stomach hit the floor. Now I understood. Agatha was truly a monster.

"Alcohol," Cranky Reed said. "After that story we need alcohol."

"On it." Jezelle exited the room and returned with a bottle of whiskey and a tray full of shot glasses. She set the tray on the desk and poured out half the bottle. Bram picked up a shot and brought it to me. "Do you understand now why I fear for your safety if you spend time with that woman?"

I nodded.

"Good." He handed me the whiskey. I downed it so fast I didn't taste it.

"Holy crap. What should I do if she calls and asks me to go for coffee again?"

"Find a polite, plausible way to decline," he said.

Bram took a shot and passed me another one.

Once we were all a bit numb, I said, "We are supposed to be figuring out who would benefit from splitting people and manipulating them." I pointed at

Cranky Reed. "Is there anything you'd do as your angry self that you wouldn't normally do?"

"Threaten to kick Sadie, apparently, which I feel terrible about." He leaned against the wall. "I apologized, but that doesn't feel like enough."

"Liquor," Jezelle said. "We have one of the largest storerooms of liquor on Main Street. Maybe someone wanted access to a special bottle of whiskey?"

"Restaurants have certain vintages of wine," I said. "Do we have anything rare enough for someone to split Reed?"

Jezelle pulled a key ring from her pocket. "As the new owner, it's time you had the full tour. Follow me and watch your step. The stairs are old and narrow."

Stairs? The tearoom was one story, so we must be going into a basement.

I stood and the room swayed. Not good. Bram came up alongside me and held out his arm. "May I escort you into the basement?"

"Will you keep me from falling down the stairs?" I asked.

"Most assuredly." He smiled at me, and my heart fluttered. "If you trip, I can always take flight to keep you from falling."

I blinked and fought the urge to sigh. Now was not the time to go all mushy over a guy. "Thanks."

"I could dose you to sobriety," Jezelle offered.

"Nope," I said. "Kind of enjoying the numbness for now."

We followed Jezelle to the back storage room and down the basement steps. I held onto the handrail with my left hand and Bram with my right. The wooden steps creaked as we descended.

The bare bulb at the top of the stairs didn't illuminate the room beyond. Same with the light at the bottom of the steps. Jezelle headed into the shadows and flipped a switch. Light poured into the room and blasted my eyeballs. I slapped a hand over my eyes. "A little warning would have been nice."

"Sorry." Jezelle said.

"You need to see this." Bram touched my shoulder.

I lowered my hand. As my pupils adjusted, my brain spun. There were aisles of shelves, set up like a liquor store. Every shelf held at least twenty bottles. The room went back at least fifty feet. "What the heck?"

Happy Reed chuckled. "Mystic Hills has been around a long time. We've imported alcohol from all over the world for decades. We don't specialize in wine, but we have some rare whiskeys, hard to find ales, you get the idea."

"Is this common knowledge?" I asked.

"No." Bram chuckled. "No, it is not."

"We supply some of the restaurants with alcohol," Jezelle said.

Cranky Reed walked across the room and moved a few bottles around on a shelf until he found what he wanted. He came back and held it out like he was presenting it at show and tell. "Maybe Sadie would like this Smoked Salmon flavored Vodka."

I cringed. "Why would someone make that?"

"Good question," Bram said. "Another question. How often do you run an inventory check? Would you know if something was missing?"

"The more expensive bottles are guarded by spells." Jezelle gestured to the right half of the room. "We run inventory spells, created by different witches twice a year."

"Are the results always the same?" I asked.

"Most of the time. The occasional error is usually due to misnaming an item. Like all Bourbon is whiskey, but not all whiskey is bourbon."

Maybe I should care about why that was, but right now it didn't seem important. "So, nothing is missing. There's nothing here that someone would split Reed to try and get a bargain on?"

"Not that I can think of," Happy Reed said.

We reconvened upstairs. My stomach growled, and I checked the time. "I don't usually drink whiskey for dinner. My stomach doesn't seem to appreciate it."

"You're in no condition to drive," Bram said.

"Are you?" I asked, pretty sure I knew the answer.

"I could portal you home," he offered.

"Nope," Jezelle said. "Wait right here."

She came back a minute later with shot glasses full of pink liquid. "Anyone who wants to sober up, this is your drink."

I took one and sipped the same ginger ale taste I'd experienced before.

Bram frowned. "Who made this potion for you?"

"Yelena keeps me stocked." She shrugged.

"Of course she does." Bram downed his drink and then frowned. "I shouldn't have said that out loud."

I grinned. "That's the first sign I've seen you're not perfect."

He snorted. "You have no idea."

I liked this playful side of Bram. "Want to grab a pizza before I drive you home?" I asked trying to keep it casual.

"I'd like that."

The Pizza Place was not an original name for a pizza restaurant, but the decor was done in soothing nature colors, and the food was excellent.

I took a bite of pepperoni pizza. It was spicy, stretchy cheese covered bliss. "This is amazing."

"It's a guilty pleasure. I try to eat healthy most of the time, but I come here once a week to indulge."

"More like twice a week," our waitress, an older woman with wings said, as she came to check on us. "Need anything else?"

"No. The pizza is delicious."

"Special Fairy seasonings." She wiggled her eyebrows and walked away.

I took another bite, and that's when I noticed something was off. I seemed to be the object of unusual attention. Was I imagining it? A quick check of the room proved my instincts were correct. People sitting at the surrounding tables stared at me. Why? Was I the only one without wings? No. There was a table of six regular humans in corner.

"What did I do to deserve this much attention? It's not like I'm the only one without wings." I nodded toward the table in the corner.

Bram glanced around and then smiled. "Believe me, they have wings, just not in their current form."

I waited. He didn't fill me in. "You're just going to leave me hanging?"

He leaned closer. "They are a spectacular race."

"Okay." I waited for him to fill in the rest of the blanks. He didn't. "Go on."

"They're shifters."

I glared at him. "That's nice and vague."

He leaned in and whispered, "Dragon shifters."

"What?" I said a little too loudly.

He laughed.

"Are you kidding me?" I asked.

"No. I must admit I'm envious of their wings. Mine are functional, but theirs are remarkable, and they have the most interesting breath weapons."

He couldn't mean... "fire...they breathe fire?"

"Fire, ice, wind, seismic waves, and lighting," he said.

I blinked while I tried to take all of this in. "That's amazing. Are they dangerous?"

"Given their strength, they could be. Some citizens of Mystic Hills weren't thrilled when they joined the community, but under the Laws of Sanctuary all magical creatures are allowed to live here. Regarding your earlier question, while humans sometimes eat here, you are the only flightless individual here at the moment."

"Flightless?" I grinned. "That's a funny term."

"Wings are an important part of our culture, so it's a distinction we sometimes make. Unlike the witches, we don't believe ourselves to be above others, just different."

If a human married a fairy would their children have wings? That was not a first date kind of question. Not that this was a date. Or maybe it was. Either way I didn't want Bram to think I was auditioning for the role of his baby mama.

"What's going on in your head?" Bram asked.

I took another bite before answering. "All sorts of things. I'm wondering about the twins, thinking about witch politics, and considering ordering a pizza to take home for Sadie, Victor, Dave, and Celia."

"Do you enjoy living with roommates?" Bram asked.

"I never thought about it. They belong in the house as much, if not more, than I do, so I'd never ask them to leave. I'd probably be lonely without them."

"I like my quiet time," he said.

I could relate. "When I first started working in preschool, it took a while to get used to the noise. A creative, happy classroom is full of kids laughing and talking and more often than not, screaming. I craved silence on the drive home from work so I could decompress. One of my friends wanted to carpool to save money. I told her we could, but when she started talking, I pointed to the clock and said, 'It's quiet time.' She was shocked and then she laughed."

"And did she honor your quiet time on the drive home?"

"For the most part, yes. After a few months, I adjusted to the noise level, and I didn't mind talking on the way home, but I still wouldn't let her play music."

We'd just received the bill when Bram's phone rang. He answered and said, "Yes. I'll be right there." He pulled money from his wallet and placed it on the table. "I'm sorry. I have to go."

"I understand. I hope the person is okay."

Amusement shown from his eyes. "Some young witches go a little wild with their magic. Eventually it catches up to them in the form of a minor injury." With that, he opened a portal and stepped through it.

Everyone turned to me. My face heated. "Sorry to disturb your dinner. He's a Healer. He had to go."

The waitress came back to the table with a box. "Here you are." She picked up the money Bram left. "Need anything else?"

"Can I have a large cheese pizza to go?" I asked.

"Here." She handed me a paper menu. "Order from your house and it will be fresh for your family."

"Thank you." Did she mean carry out or could Lilly order for me? I had no idea but this was definitely my cue to leave.

CHAPTER 10

The next morning I sat at the kitchen table, eating cold pizza for breakfast.

Victor entered the room, and his brow creased. He pointed at my plate. "That is disgusting."

I laughed. "Cold pizza for breakfast was a college staple. I haven't eaten it in a long time."

He poured himself a cup of coffee and joined me. "I heard from both Reeds this morning. Their personalities have leveled out."

"He seemed much better yesterday. Did he share how they balanced themselves?" I was dying to know.

"No." He gestured at me with his coffee cup. "I can tell from your expression you're as curious as I am. He wouldn't share any details."

"Maybe they talked out Cranky Reed's issues, and I'm fairly certain I was at the top of the list."

Victor pressed his lips together in a thin line and shook his head. "Your mother should have kept her word and brought you back to Mystic Hills. Both you and Reed should have been allowed to make a choice. Maybe you'd still be together, maybe you wouldn't, but she had no right to do that to you or him."

"Agreed. I'm still trying to figure out how not to resent her. I love her because she's my mom, but I hate what she did."

Celia poked her head into the room. "Sorry to eavesdrop, but sometimes you have to separate the person from their bad decision."

"That's not always easy to do," Victor said.

"I think you have to see if the good outweighs the bad." She flew over and landed on the kitchen table. "Lilly, may I have toast with strawberry basal jam and a cup of green tea please?"

A miniature piece of toast appeared on a saucer next to a thimble full of tea. "Thank you." Celia sat cross legged on the table and took a bite of her toast.

"We should go shopping for a miniature tea set." I glanced at Victor. "I'm assuming little girls in Mystic Hills have tea parties."

"I'm fairly certain that tea parties are a universal cross species activity for girls," Victor said.

"We should go see Orville," Celia declared. "He has some lovely tea party sets. I can visit with him and then we'll pick out dishes for while I'm staying with you."

"Lilly could order a set," Victor said.

"Then we wouldn't have a reason to visit my friend." Celia sipped her tea. "I like to check in on him. I worry about him since his wife passed."

"I didn't realize he was widowed," I said.

She hugged the thimble of hot tea to her chest. "It's been three years. At first, he was inconsolable. He occupies his time with the shop. It allows him to be social. I know he can be difficult to get along with at times, but he's a good man."

Did Celia care for Orville as more than a friend? Could Sprites and humans be involved or was this a friendship? Chalk that up as another question to add to the many I already had.

When we walked into Orville's Oddities I recognized Mrs. Fairbanks waiting impatiently with her arms crossed and tapping her right foot while Mr. Orville helped a young man with a train set.

Celia flew up on my shoulder and whispered, "That woman is not to be trusted."

I nodded rather than saying anything out loud, since Mrs. Fairbanks was so well connected. It was probably a good idea to put some distance between ourselves and the crabby woman. "Let's go find some tea sets."

Celia flitted through the air from table to table while I wandered, checking out our options. There was a green set with grapes which didn't appeal to me. I found another set with blue jays. Not what I had in mind. Finally I spotted tiny white dishes with pink and yellow flowers. They reminded me of a set I'd had and loved as a kid. A note taped to the box explained one of the plates was missing. I didn't think Celia would mind.

"Give me my grandmother's ring right now." Mrs. Fairbanks voice echoed through the room. "Or you will suffer the consequences."

Uh-oh. I turned around. The unpleasant woman stood inches from Orville who appeared unbothered by her threat.

"Mrs. Fairbanks, such behavior is unbecoming to a woman of your social status. I explained to you, quite clearly, that you may purchase the ring for a reasonable price. I paid your former daughter-in-law a few thousand less than the price I'm offering you. I'm just a business man looking to make a minimal profit. As a successful business woman you must be able to understand my position."

"Give me the ring or I'll report it stolen. You'll be shut down for selling illegal goods."

Celia zipped over and stood on Orville's right shoulder. "You will do no such thing unless you want all your flowers to shrivel and blacken. How stately will your houses appear once your lawns and landscaping are nothing but piles of rotting vegetation."

That odd threat must have worked because Mrs. Fairbanks backed up a step. "Fine. The truth is my son has tied up most of our cash assets at the moment due to his divorce. If he'd listened to me and married an appropriate partner we wouldn't be in this situation, and I wouldn't be in such a foul mood. Will you accept payment in blood? I've recently come into a surplus, which I planned to use in my spells, but I'd be willing to give it to you."

"Give me a moment to figure out the conversion of dollars to pints." He walked around behind his cash register and pulled out a calculator. After hitting a few buttons, his eyes widened. He grabbed a piece of paper and wrote the number down on it before passing it to Mrs. Fairbanks. "I'll accept payments in installments since it might be hard to transport all of that at once."

My mouth went dry. She had extra blood right after Violet had been drained? Something told me that might not be a coincidence. In the real world I could report this conversation to the police, and they might look into it. In Mystic Hills, Mrs. Fairbanks seemed untouchable.

"If you'll write up a blood contract stating those terms, I can have the bank transfer payment from my account to yours by the end of the week."

Orville walked behind his desk and opened a drawer. He paged through some files until he found the one he wanted. He retrieved a packet of papers with a flourish. "Here we are."

Did everyone in Mystic hills keep blood contracts on hand? That seemed...creepy.

Using slow methodical pen strokes, he filled in numbers and names and then pushed the paper across the counter toward Mrs. Fairbanks. She read the document and signed in one giant swoosh. He added his signature and then set the pages in a black leather binder which he sprinkled with something that looked like salt. A light smoky scent drifted through the air. When he opened the binder two copies sat side by side.

"I haven't seen a spelled copier like that since I was a child," Mrs. Fairbanks said.

"It was my fathers. Works every time," Orville said. "Sometimes the old ways are the best."

"And my ring?" Mrs. Fairbanks said like she expected him to hand it over right then and there.

He gave her a patient smile. "Once the funds are deposited, I'll hand deliver it to your doorstep."

She nodded and left.

The shop door closed, signaling she was gone. Orville sat on the stool behind the counter and sighed. "That was interesting."

"She is frightening," I said.

"I didn't like her threatening you," Celia said. "I'm glad you didn't give her the ring."

"I'm so happy you stopped by for a visit." He pointed at the tea set I held. "Is that for my dear friend?"

"Yes."

"Then it's on the house. If you don't mind, I'd love to visit with Celia. She could meet you at home after we're done."

Apparently I wasn't invited to stay. "Sounds perfect. I'll take the tea set with me and see you later."

———— ◈ ————

I exited the store and decided to take a walk down Main Street. It would be hot by the afternoon, but right now it was comfortably warm and the sun was shining. The sweet scent of baked goods drifted through the air along with the robust smell of freshly ground coffee beans.

I put the teaset in my car and then headed for *The Bakers Dozen*. Their cinnamon scones were amazing. Maybe I'd grab a coffee and a treat and sit outside at one of their patio tables. As I came closer to the restaurant, I noticed most of the white wrought iron seating was taken. When I pushed the door open, the scent of fresh from the oven chocolate chip cookies made my mouth water. Maybe I should change my order.

I stood in line behind three women and waited my turn. Such a contrast in how these people waited and how Mrs. Fairbanks had acted. I never understood people who thought the world revolved around them. If a preschooler could learn to wait their turn, then why couldn't a full grown adult?

When I reached the counter, Grace Stewart, the owner smiled at me. "Hello, Belinda. What can I get for you?"

I scanned the case of baked goods. Muffins and scones in every variety sat next to donuts draped in icing. Everything looked wonderful, but there weren't any cookies. That was a puzzle. "What smells like chocolate chip cookies?"

"That lovely aroma would be the chocolate chip muffins. One of my personal favorites."

"Sounds good. I'll have one of those and a large cup of French vanilla coffee."

I paid and then checked out my seating options. A few of the tables outside had cleared, so I headed toward the door. I was almost there, when someone called my name. I glanced over and saw Agatha seated at a table by herself.

"Why don't you join me?" she said.

Uh-oh. What should I do? Panic skittered up my spine. I didn't want to make small talk with Agatha but I definitely didn't want to tick her off. I gave her the most genuine smile I could muster as I crossed the space between us.

When I didn't sit right away, she frowned. "I can tell by your expression that someone has been telling tales about me."

Crud. How did I say this tactfully? I swallowed hard. "Your hexes are terrifying."

"They are. And for good reason." She gestured at the chair. "Sit and allow me to explain myself."

Since I didn't want to be on the receiving end of one of those hexes, I sat.

She leaned toward me. "I don't accept all the clients who come to me. I don't exact revenge on jilted lovers or settle family disputes. I only punish those who truly deserve it."

I unwrapped my muffin. "Like the man who cheated on his wife and impregnated two other witches?"

She shook her head. "Poor Bram. Witnessing that man's suffering scarred him. What he didn't know was why I went to such extreme measures."

I expected her to continue. She didn't. I guess she was giving me the chance to understand her or to walk away. I wanted to give her the benefit of the doubt, so I stayed. "Why did you make it so horrific?"

"You know blood is the basis for all magic in Mystic Hills."

I took a bite of my muffin and nodded.

"There is a singular type of blood that holds more power than any other. The blood of a newborn babe, less than an hour old, allows a witch to craft spells of amazing power."

She stared at me like she was waiting for me to connect the dots. I swallowed the muffin without tasting it. "A newborn's blood?" The thought turned my stomach. "Are you saying he impregnated those witches so he could drain their babies?"

"That is exactly what I'm saying. He told both women that the child was stillborn. It's the same line he used on his wife once he had his desired heir."

A wave of nausea rolled over me. "His poor wife. Those poor women. How could anyone do that?"

"He was truly evil," Agatha said. "And he deserved a punishment that fit his horrendous crimes." She tilted her head and studied me. "Do you agree?"

Tears filled my eyes, but I nodded. "He deserved that and worse."

"Now that you understand, I'll leave you to your coffee." She stood to leave.

"Agatha, wait."

She paused.

"I'm sorry I believed the worst of you. Stay and talk with me?"

"Why?" she asked.

"Because I need more friends, and I think you do too."

She sat back down. "I've had the same friends for fifty years. It's about time I added someone new to the list."

I took a bite of my muffin. The brown sugar and vanilla flavor combined with the chocolate chips made my taste buds do a happy dance. "This might be the best muffin I've ever tasted."

"Have you had her maple bacon muffins?"

"No, but they sound amazing."

We chatted about baked goods and coffee and the weather until she glanced at her watch. "This has been lovely. I have an appointment at the bank. I should be going." She reached over and touched my hand. "You can share what I told you with Bram. It may change his mind about me or it may not." With that she left.

I felt bad about my reaction to Agatha. How could anyone spend their life crafting such vile hexes? Then again, maybe her services were needed. That was a disturbing thought.

I finished off my coffee. What should I do with the rest of my day? I glanced at the donut shaped clock behind the counter. It was only ten-thirty. Maybe I'd head to *Tea & Spirits* to see if anyone wanted to speak to the spirit of their dearly departed. If not, maybe I'd call Aunt Teresa's spirit. It'd been a while since I'd spoken to her.

Another person I hadn't spoken to was Yelena. The librarian derailed my first visit, and Violet's ghost derailed Bram and I from asking Yelena if she'd figured out a spell. Would today be a third strike, or would I be able to talk to the woman who might be able to solve this entire problem?

The walk to her store took less than ten minutes. When I opened the door, Yelena stood behind her cash register.

"Belinda, you're just the person I wanted to talk to."

I approached her and leaned on the counter. "Likewise. Have you made any progress with those spells that should recombine the twins?"

"No." She tapped her nails on the glass. "It's quite vexing. The only theory I've come up with is there is nothing to heal because while the individuals are split in two, they are not, in fact, ill."

"Bram and I discussed that theory yesterday. He's quite annoyed."

Her tapping on the glass stopped abruptly, and then it started again. "If you'd told me he'd figured it out, I would have thrown a fit." She brushed silver tendrils of her hair behind her ear. "That sounds immature, but it's the truth. He's gifted. He's not supposed to be able to create spells."

I had been right about the professional jealousy. "His gift is using people's blood and other ingredients to heal them. I'm sure there are many spells you can perform which are beyond his ability."

"You're right," she said. "There are. Now what are you planning to do next about the twins?"

"I'd hoped you'd have some ideas on how to recombine them."

"Not a single one," she admitted.

Ugh. "Okay, then I need to figure out who would gain from splitting people in two."

"How do you plan to do that?"

"With stubborn determination," I said.

She gave a sad smile. "Your Aunt Teresa was a force to be reckoned with, too."

"I'm going to visit her spirit at the tearoom today. Maybe she'll have some suggestion on how to solve this puzzle."

Tea & Spirits was mostly empty. I nodded at the women sprinkled around the room in small groups and walked over to the bar where Jezelle stood cutting up a lemon. The scent of lemon zest filled the air.

"Good morning." She poured me a glass of sweet iced tea and added a slice of the fresh lemon.

"Thank you." I took a sip. As usual, the sugar to tea ratio was perfect.

"What are your plans for today?" Jezelle asked.

"I thought I'd see if anyone wanted to speak with a spirit."

"For that, you'll want the evening crowd. These ladies are here for real world gossip."

"Hear anything interesting?"

Jezelle scooped the lemon wedges into a plastic container and set it on the bar. "Mrs. Fairbanks visited the bank and is planning to pay someone with a large amount of blood. No one is sure why."

News traveled fast in this town. "I know why."

She leaned on the bar. "Spill the tea, please."

"Violet sold her wedding ring set to Orville, and Mrs. Fairbanks is buying it back."

Jezelle laughed. "I would not want to be on the wrong side of that woman."

"She's scary," I admitted.

"Can I share your story with the class?" Jezelle gestured towards the women.

"Don't say it's from me, but sure, have fun with it."

I went into Reed's office and found both of them sitting at the desk, which made my brain spin for a moment.

"What?" they said in unison.

"Sorry, just passing through to my tiny office. I didn't expect both of you to be here."

One Reed stood, picked up his chair, and said, "We borrowed this from you. I'll grab another one."

Once I was in my office seated in my newly returned chair, I said, "Aunt Teresa, do you have time to talk?"

She swirled into existence and smiled at me. "Hello, dear, it's been a while. How are you?"

"Pretty good. There's a mystery I need help solving." I told her about the twins.

"That is interesting. So you need to figure out who set this in motion so they can put the twins back together?"

"Yes. I wish I knew how to do that."

She frowned. "The people who did this must need something from someone. Once they get what they want, they should end the spell and change everyone back."

"So, we should just let it run its course?" I asked. "What if they don't care about changing people back?"

"I didn't think of that. Whoever did this is dangerous. Make sure you don't go investigating on your own. Take one of the Reeds."

I snorted.

"Oh dear. Things aren't going well between you two?"

"Actually I think we're on the road to being friends. It's severely awkward at times, but it's good."

"Just friends? Why? Is he dating someone?"

"Jezelle. They've been together about six months."

"Really?" She laughed. "They hid it well. I had no idea."

"I've been spending time with Bram," I offered, hoping to see what she thought of him.

"Bram is a fairy." She stated this fact like it I might not have noticed.

"Yeah, his wings kind of give that away."

She swirled for a moment, and then came back into focus. "Jezelle's parents did not have an easy time of it in the beginning. Almost everyone accepts them now. Just be aware, if you fall for him there are those who will not approve."

"I didn't think it was an issue." I honestly hadn't. Since everyone seemed to like Jezelle, I didn't think people cared about cross-species dating.

"Maybe it's not. I just want you to be happy. If he makes you happy, go for it. Anything else going on that I should know about?"

I told her about Celia coming home with me.

"She was a wonderful houseguest. I'm sure the cats are thrilled to spend time with her."

My phone rang, interrupting our conversation. "Sorry. Let me see who this is." I flipped my phone open. "Hello?"

"Hello, I was wondering if you'd like to help me solve a puzzle." Bram's melodious voice flowed through the phone.

"Sure. What type of puzzle?"

"I'm at Violet's new home. Can you come and meet me, or would you like me to portal you here?"

"I have my car. Let me say goodbye to my aunt, and I'll meet you there in fifteen minutes."

"So that was Bram." My aunt wiggled her eyebrows.

"He needs my help with something."

CHAPTER 11

Violet's yellow house basked in the sunshine when I parked in her driveway. Before I reached the front door, Bram opened it.

"I hope you can confirm my suspicions." The concern on his face was offset by the wide grin he gave me. "I believe we have an invisible guest."

"I'll do my best." I entered the house, walked into the living room, and saw Violet and her mom sitting on the couch. Ghost Violet swirled in the corner by a plant stand.

"There you are." Ghost Violet swooped toward me.

"Hello, Ghost Violet."

"I knew it," Bram said.

"Give the man a prize," Ghost Violet snarled.

"Please calm down," I tried to use a soothing tone. "I promise we are trying to help you."

"She's been shaking picture frames and breaking glass," Mrs. Kingsley, Violet's mom, said. "I cut my hand cleaning up a broken tea pitcher."

"That's where you came in?" I pointed to Bram.

He nodded. "The cut was too deep for a standard healing spell. Can you convince Violet to stop this behavior before someone else is hurt?"

"I'll try." How could I talk her down? I'd start with reason. "Ghost Violet, if you keep acting out you're on your way to becoming a vengeful spirit."

Her responding scream echoed off the walls and made the pictures frames rattle.

That didn't work. Time to pull out the teacher voice. "That's enough, Violet. If you continue this behavior, you're going to hurt yourself and your friends. I need you to take a minute, calm yourself, and listen to my words."

Violet shimmered and stilled. "I'm listening."

"If you were the ghost of someone who died, I'd convince you to move on. But you aren't moving on. You're staying here while we figure out how to recombine all the twins. Once we find out who started this, we can reverse it and return you and everyone else to their bodies."

"It's her." Ghost Violet shimmered and then solidified. "My mother-in-law drained me."

I told the others what she'd said.

"As much as I resent her for destroying my marriage, I can't see her doing that," real-life Violet said.

"She was there. We had coffee," Ghost Violet said.

"What about after the coffee?" I asked. "Was there anyone else?"

Ghost Violet pulsed like a strobe light. "There were flowers. I thought they were from Herb."

"Who sent them?" I asked.

"Sent what?" Bram asked.

"Ghost Violet remembers flowers. If they were delivered, they should have a card," I said. "Maybe it will give us a clue."

"I still have a key," regular Violet said. "I can't go with you, but you could go inside."

"We should portal in," Bram said. "That way, no one will know we're there."

I grinned. "Look at you being all sneaky."

"I have my moments." He took my hand. "Hold on tight. I'd hate to lose you in the void."

"What?" I clutched his hand tighter.

He pointed at me and laughed. "You should see your face."

"Not funny." I clamped onto his arm with other free hand for good measure. Plus I didn't mind holding onto him.

He said a spell I couldn't quite make out and waved his free hand in a circular motion. An oval shaped portal appeared. A beautiful kitchen with floor to ceiling cabinets lining one wall came into view.

We stepped through, and I experienced a rare case of kitchen lust. Not for Bram, but for the white Carrara marble countertops veined with gold, the restaurant-grade appliances, and the subway tiled backsplash. I ran my hand over the nearest countertop. It felt like silk.

Bram headed straight for the crystal vase of what appeared to be two dozen long stemmed yellow, white, and pink roses on the kitchen table. "Impressive flowers."

I'd only seen arrangements like that on television. "If someone wanted her to think they were from Herb, they'd have to be expensive."

"True." He pulled out the tube of magic glitter gel that protected his skin from spells and applied some to his hands. "Let's see if there is a card." He searched through the flowers until he found a small card on a ribbon. His face hardened as he read the message.

"What does it say?"

"If you're reading this, she's already drained."

My stomach dropped to the floor. "What the heck?"

"It would appear someone has a sick sense of humor. They must have dressed as a flower delivery person. The flowers would be quite heavy. Whoever it was carried them into the house."

"I know ghost Violet has been a pain, but I hate that someone gave her hope Herb might want to reconcile and it was just a distraction to drain her."

"And with the new law, no one will pursue whoever committed this crime."

I didn't understand. "They left her dead on the tile floor, that's against the new law."

"But her other half is still alive, so legally Violet Fairbanks isn't dead."

A strange idea invaded my brain. "If I go along with your twisted logic, do you think the person who did this knew about the twin problem? If they did does that mean other twins are in danger or was this aimed at Violet?"

"Those are all good questions. Unfortunately, I don't have any answers."

Bram portaled us back to Violet's new house. We told them what we'd found.

Ghost Violet pulsed with anger. "I forgot about the delivery man. The flowers arrived after my mother-in-law."

"What did your mother-in-law want?" I asked. She must have had a motive to visit her soon to be ex daughter-in-law.

Her image flickered and then calmed. "She informed me that if I wanted to remarry, I wouldn't have trouble conceiving. Previously I'd been told I was the reason Herb and I weren't able to have children. That evil woman dosed Herb with something to keep him infertile because she didn't want grandchildren with mixed blood."

My chest ached and tears filled my eyes. "I'm so sorry." Mrs. Fairbanks was a horrible human being.

"What?" Human Violet's gaze locked onto mine. "What did she say?"

I explained what her mother-in-law had done and why she hadn't been able to have children.

No one spoke for a moment. Tears ran down Violet's face.

Mrs. Kingsley scooted over on the couch and pulled her daughter into a hug. "Karma will come for that woman one day. Maybe it's for the best. You can truly start over with no ties to that evil family."

"Sometimes a person's punishment is that they continue living their lives as their awful unhappy selves," Bram offered.

"I'm not sure that is punishment enough." Human Violet sat up, grabbed a tissue from the coffee table and dried her face. "Ghost Violet, I promise I'll let you back in as soon as someone figures out how to recombine us."

"Thank you," Ghost Violet said. "Can you leave a television on in one of the rooms? If I have something else to focus on, I might not freak out so much."

I relayed the message.

"Of course." Violet stood. "Bram, Belinda, thank you for your help. I'm going to take my other half upstairs to the spare bedroom so she can watch some movies."

After Violet left the room, Mrs. Kingsley sighed. "That Fairbanks woman tried to bribe me into talking Violet out of marrying her precious son. Now I wish I'd taken the money and done as she asked. It would have saved Violet years of heart break."

I kind of understand why Agatha's hexes might be needed.

"We'll leave you for now," Bram said. "This probably goes without saying, but don't let in any strangers, especially if they have flowers."

"We'll put the house on lockdown after you leave," she responded.

As we walked out the door, I noticed my car was the only one in the driveway. "Do you want a ride home or were you going to use a portal?"

"I'd appreciate a ride to my office. It's off main street past the bank."

His office sat next to a bookstore. I parked in front of it. "Do you spend your lunch hours browsing for books?" That's what I would do.

"Sometimes. They have excellent tea. Would like to join me for a cup?"

"Sure."

The store had an interesting assortment of books. A display of journals caught my eye. I picked up a yellow leather one embossed with sunflowers and another one with a paper turquoise cover with the word *Memories* written across the front in gold calligraphy. The paper in both was a decent weight. I checked their prices and then noticed the buy one get one half off sign. "I might need both of these."

Bram smiled. "I love a good journal."

As if he could be more perfect.

A small cafe area in the back of the store held three wicker tables. Two were already occupied.

"Why don't you sit while I grab our drinks," Bram suggested.

"Good idea." I sat and leafed through the journal. Some pages were lined, and others were blank. That was different. I suppose you could write on some pages and draw on others.

Bram joined me at the table with two cups of hot water, a small tray of individually wrapped tea bags, and a large cup of ice.

"One of the reasons I enjoy this establishment is they give you the option of hot or iced tea without judgement."

"Some places judge you for wanting iced tea in the summer?" I picked lemon cranberry tea bag and put it in my cup to steep.

"Yes. My grandmother favored a tea shop that only served hot tea because that's the way it was meant to be served."

"I didn't realize that was an issue. Before I forget to mention it, I stopped by Yelena's shop. She hasn't been able to create a spell to combine the people who are split apart. She came to the same conclusion you did. The twins aren't ill."

"Did I figure it out before her?" he asked.

"I believe you did."

He smiled. "Is it wrong that I'm basking in the glow of understanding something before her?"

"No comment." I laughed.

Bram looked so pleased with himself. His eyes were bright, his bronze skin glowed, and he was so darn handsome.

Did I have a shot with him? I wasn't sure. There was something I needed to know before I pursued this line of romantic thought. It might be awkward, but if I asked the right way, maybe it wouldn't be. "Violet's situation reminded me of Jezelle and the boyfriend who rejected her because she was only half fairy."

"There are similarities." Bram dumped half the ice into his tea, leaving the other half for me.

He didn't expound on the situation. I tried again while I let my tea steep a bit longer. "Jezelle is mixed race, and she's one of the first people I met in Mystic Hills. I didn't think mixed race marriages and children were an issue."

"Mystic Hills has always been home to a diverse population. A hundred years ago everyone kept to their own kind. Fifty years ago diverse marriages caused a scandal. Every decade since then people have adjusted to the idea, maybe because there are more mixed race people walking around. Today I believe most people, except for the witches, don't blink an eye at a mixed race marriage."

I added ice to my cup and sipped. It was refreshing but weak. I'd hoped for more of a lemonade flavor. "How did Jezelle's mother and father meet?"

"My aunt is widely recognized as one of the great beauties of fairy kind. My mother is beautiful by any standard, but her sister was ethereal."

I laughed. "I've thought that about Jezelle before."

"Rightly so," he said. "Jezelle's mother couldn't go anywhere without men approaching her. Male fairies vied for her attention. She noticed a human, an artist, who was constantly around. He would smile and nod to acknowledge her but never spoke. One day, she sought him out and asked what he was working on. He was shy and refused to show her his drawings. A week later she followed him home and snuck into the barn which he used as a gallery. There were depictions of her everywhere, from sketches to watercolors and oil paintings."

"He discovered her in the barn and apologized for what she'd found. He declared she was the most beautiful creature he'd ever seen, and he couldn't imagine wanting to draw or paint another likeness because they all paled in comparison to her loveliness."

I sucked in a breath. "Wow." If any guy ever said that to me, which he wouldn't but if he did...I sighed. "That's the most romantic thing I've ever heard."

Bram laughed. "She had a similar reaction to his declaration. They started dating soon after and were married within the year much to the dismay of hopeful males everywhere."

"That is such a good story. Please tell me they're still happily married."

"Indeed, they are," he assured me.

I hadn't realized how much I needed to hear a real life happily-ever-after. "My faith in true love is restored."

He shook his head and sipped his tea.

"What, you don't believe in love that stands the test of time?"

"I do. I just haven't seen many examples of it recently."

Another question nagged my brain. "Even though Jezelle is half fairy, she has wings. By looking at her no one would know she wasn't full fairy so why did her ex-boyfriend care?"

"Because he and his family are purists."

"This may be in inappropriate question, but scientifically speaking, could Jezelle have been born without wings?"

"No. For some reason wings trump flightless genetics every time."

"Kind of like dark hair trumps blond hair?"

"Yes. Fairies genetic makeup isn't much different from humans to start with. It's like evolution took a slightly different path to end up with wings. The way humans and fairies are raised and the beliefs they are taught can be quite different depending on their upbringing. Some fairies believe themselves superior to the flightless, while some humans look down on anyone with non-human characteristics."

"No matter the race, there are always some ignorant, entitled people."

"I'm afraid that is a universal truth." He checked his watch. "I have an appointment soon. I should be going. Thanks for your help today with Violet."

My first instinct was to say, no worries, but some people didn't care for that phrase, so I went with, "You're welcome."

He headed for the door, and I watched every step he took, admiring his broad shoulders and his wings which glistened in the light.

A silver haired woman who'd been reading at a nearby table turned to me. "He's a handsome one."

I smiled. "Yes, he is."

"Back in my day, I never would have considered dating a fairy. If he'd been around and interested, I might have changed my mind."

Was he interested? I wasn't sure. I hoped so, but I'd never seen him be anything but kind to other people unless they were rude first. Maybe what I thought of as flirting was his normal demeanor. "I can't tell if he's interested or not. What do you think?"

"I think he is, but there's only one person you can ask and get a reliable answer."

I picked up my journals. "I'm not ready to take that leap yet."

She laughed and went back to her book. I purchased the journals and headed home.

Two cats and a sprite greeted me when I walked into the house, which sounded like the set up for a weird joke.

"Did you have fun with Orville?" I asked Celia.

"We had a lovely visit."

"How about you?" Sadie asked. "What have you been up to?"

"It's been a busy afternoon." I told her about my visit with Agatha and what I'd learned about her hexes.

"Draining newborns?" Sadie's fur stood on end. "That man deserved so much worse. Did you tell Bram?"

"No. I was too busy helping with Violet." I shared the story about Violet's evil mother-in-law and how she'd fooled Violet into thinking it was her fault she couldn't conceive.

Celia buzzed around in circles. "One day someone will pay Mrs. Fairbanks back for all her unkindness, and I hope I'm there to help."

"What Mrs. Fairbanks did is reprehensible, but what type of psycho drains a person and leaves a card bragging about it?" Dave asked.

"I have no idea. On a positive note, I had tea with Bram, and he told me the most romantic story." I relayed the tale of Jezelle's parents and what her dad said to her mom.

Sadie and Celia sighed like I had. Dave huffed out a breath. "How are the rest of us males supposed to compete with that declaration of love?"

"I'm sure you'll think of something," Sadie told him.

"I'm doomed," Dave declared.

"Not all women need pretty words. Actions show feelings, too." Celia flew up and looked around. "Did you bring in my pretty new tea set?"

"I left it in the car with my journals. I'll go get them."

"Did that handsome Healer scramble your brain?" Celia teased.

"That obvious, huh?"

CHAPTER 12

After retrieving the items from my car, I left Celia and the cats in the kitchen to have a tea party while I grabbed a pen and went up to my room. Sitting cross-legged on my bed I ran my fingers over the butter soft leather of the yellow journal.

I opened it, breaking the spine. Journals that wouldn't stay open annoyed me. I was sure that would horrify true bibliophiles, but you couldn't write in a journal if you couldn't open it all the way. I tapped the pen on the cream colored paper. What did I want to write? I wrote down the names of all the twins and then added people I should be wary of and those I trusted. Funnily enough, I trusted Agatha. I only semi-trusted Orville, but Celia believed in him. I was definitely wary of the Fairbanks, both mother and son. Were there other sketchy people involved in this situation?

Could this whole thing revolve around the Fairbanks somehow? If Violet refused to sign divorce papers, would Herb or his mother go to these extremes? I wasn't sure. They were used to getting exactly what they wanted, so who knew what lengths they'd go to. Then again, I'd seen Mrs. Fairbanks throw a tantrum over a wedding ring so her reaction to possibly losing the house would be much worse.

I glanced at the other journal and ran my fingertips over the gold letters which spelled out *Memories*. I was still missing memories from my previous life in Mystic Hills. I was probably better off not remembering my relationship with Reed. It was easier to treat it like an unrequited crush rather than the loss of true love. Should I use this book like a diary to record personal feelings and events in case someone removed my memories again?

My phone rang, yanking me back to reality. I grabbed it off the nightstand where I'd plugged it in to charge. "Hello?"

"Hello, this is Lisa Laddow from the bank."

Like I wouldn't know who she was. "Hello, Lisa. What's up?"

"I need you to confirm some information. Mrs. Fairbanks reported you witnessed a blood contract signed between herself and Orville, but you didn't sign the document."

That was weird. "I shopped for a tea set while they made their deal. No one officially asked me to witness or sign anything."

"But you heard the exchange, so you could sign the document."

"Why would she want me to do that?" I wasn't involved in the exchange.

"Given the amount of blood in question, we need a third party to verify she isn't being pressured into exchanging blood for goods."

I laughed. "Do you think anyone could pressure Mrs. Fairbanks into doing anything she didn't want to do?" This was ridiculous.

"Be that as it may, I'll need you to come sign the paperwork, unless someone else was also present."

"Celia was there. She heard everything and even helped facilitate a fair exchange."

"Mrs. Fairbanks failed to mention that fact," Lisa said. "Can you ask Celia to come to the bank?"

"In place of me or in addition to?" I wasn't volunteering for anything Fairbanks related if I could avoid it.

"Either of you will do," Lisa said. "Make sure one of you comes down to the bank before close of business tomorrow or you'll both be fined."

"What?" The click of the phone set my teeth on edge. She'd hung up on me. Rude.

I stomped downstairs and shared this information with Celia and the cats.

"That's ridiculous," Sadie said.

"There's no way out of witnessing the deal," Dave said.

"I'll sign," Celia offered. "It will draw suspicion away from me when future events unfold."

"What are you planning?" I asked.

"A little anonymous revenge," Celia's wings buzzed with excitement.

"I'm not sure that's a good idea." Not that Mrs. Fairbanks didn't deserve a truckload of grief. "Anything you do will be traced back to Orville due to the paperwork." And me by extension, which I didn't need.

"I hate your logic, but I can't fault it." She flew a lap around the kitchen. "I've got it. On a random day next month, Mrs. Fairbanks will receive a flowering tree as a gift. Wherever she plants it the tree will thrive, tripling in size until it's covered in the most beautiful blood red blossoms. Wherever the petals fall a new tree will spring up growing to adult height over night. Each of its petals will birth new trees until a forest grows and chokes her lawn and landscaping and eventually blocks the very door to her home."

"As fun as that sounds, won't the trees take over the town?" I asked.

"No." Celia flew in a tight circle. "That's the beauty of the spell. The trees will only thrive on Fairbanks land."

"That's a unique form of revenge," Sadie said.

"Thank you. I can't wait to see her fawn over the tree and its blossoms until she realizes it will take over her house and seal her from her home."

"I don't suppose we could seal her inside her home?" I asked.

They all laughed. I hadn't been joking. Then I thought of something. "Please make sure it doesn't affect Violet Fairbanks new house."

"Don't worry. I'll adjust the spell to be specific for the woman who deserves it."

"Thank you."

The moral of this interaction was don't mess with a sprite.

I ended up accompanying Celia to the bank the next day to sign the papers on Dave's advice. He thought Mrs. Fairbanks might take offense if I didn't step up to do my part.

As I walked into the building, I took a moment to admire the lobby floor which was tiled to look like the night sky.

"Such a lovely piece of art," Celia said from her perch on my shoulder.

"It almost seems wrong to walk on it," I said.

"The artist designed it specifically to be tread upon," Celia pointed out.

"I never thought of it that way."

We continued on our way to Lisa's office. Her door was open. I knocked, and she glanced up. Given the way her eyebrows scrunched together in irritation, this was the workaholic version of Lisa.

"Have a seat while I get everything in order."

I sat in a brown leather chair while Celia perched on my shoulder.

Lisa read through a document and placed a red post-it note next to several lines. She shoved the contract across the desk. "Sign where I indicated."

I needed a little more explanation before I put pen to paper. "What exactly am I signing, and does it obligate me in any way?"

Lisa leaned back in her chair and looked at me like I was an idiot.

"You're under no obligation. Your signature denotes you witnessed a business deal which was entered into in good faith by both parties."

"Is this type of contract uncommon?"

"The amount of blood is unusual. Most people trade in ounces, not pints."

That brought up a disturbing question. "Why would Mrs. Fairbanks have so much blood on hand?"

Lisa leaned forward. "The wealthier families have their own refrigerated vaults full of blood. This isn't that strange."

"Do you think your other half would ask questions about this type of transaction?"

"Please, she's too busy with her boyfriend to bat an eye at any transaction." She pushed the pen toward me. "Please sign so I can take my lunch break."

If she was the other Lisa, I'd ask her to lunch, but this Lisa didn't seem social, so I signed and left.

Celia flew off to run errands. I wasn't sure if that meant working on the multiplying tree for Mrs. Fairbanks, and I was probably better off not knowing. Since I didn't have plans, I decided to pop by Bram's office. If he wasn't busy, I'd ask him to lunch. When I reached his building, a sign on the door explained he was out of the office. Maybe that meant he'd been called out to heal someone. He might be at the bookstore drinking tea and I could join him which would be much less awkward. There, I had a plan.

My plan fell apart when I entered the bookstore and Bram was nowhere in sight. Now what?

The answer was obvious since I was in a bookstore. I must need a new book. A display of paranormal fiction caught my eye. I headed over and scanned the covers. You might think since I knew magic and witches were real that books based on the supernatural would lose some of their appeal. They had not. Contemporary romances and mysteries set in the real world were entertaining, but I preferred the anything is possible feel that paranormal stories possessed.

"Can I help you find something?" A woman with a blue tipped, blond pixie cut asked.

"No. Thanks. I'm browsing for now."

"Let me know if you need anything." She walked over to another customer.

I read the back cover copy of several books and chose a couple of werewolf stories.

The woman with the pixie cut rang up my purchases. "Good choice. I love these books. The next one in the series is supposed to come out by Christmas."

"Good to know." I loved knowing another book in a series was just around the corner. Some people refused to read a series until it was complete. In my opinion they were missing the point. Reading in an ongoing series meant you always had something to look forward to.

I paid and left the bookstore. For me, one of the great joys of summer was reading all day and staying up late into the night to finish a good book. It had been a while since a book had held me captive like that, but I was always on the lookout for my next binge read.

Should I stop for lunch somewhere? Lilly could make anything I wanted so I headed back to my car. I'd barely passed Bram's office when I heard someone say my name. I turned around. He stood on the front steps. I smiled and waved. Should I go talk to him or was this just a hello sort of situation?

He came down the stairs and strode toward me. What a pleasant surprise. To keep this from being awkward, I was going to tell a little white lie for the greater good.

"What are you doing here?" he asked.

I held up my recently acquired reading material. "These books caught my eye yesterday, but I didn't buy them. Since I had to run an errand at the bank I decided to see if I really needed them."

"And you did." His eyes sparkled. "I thought I recognized a fellow reader."

"Guilty as charged."

"I was about to take my lunch break," he said. "Would you like to join me?"

"Sure."

"How do you feel about barbecue?" he asked.

"Love it."

"It's a short walk. This way." He gestured toward the right, and we walked to the corner. He glanced at the books I carried. "Are you reading about werewolves?"

"Yes. It's a funny paranormal series." He seemed amused. "What?" I held up a hand to stop him from answering. "If werewolves are real and terrifying, please don't tell me until after I've enjoyed these stories."

"They aren't real in the traditional sense. It's more like there are shifters who can turn into various furry creatures."

"You mean like lions and tigers and bears, oh my?"

"Yes. Oddly enough some shifters cover a range of canine breeds and wolves while others stick to feline creatures like cats. Some transform into anything and everything whether it has fur or scales."

"You're serious?"

"Yes." He raised an eyebrow at me. "If I was going to lie, I'd make up something far more fantastic."

"So only big lies?" We turned down a side street lined with small houses. What had once been a residential block had been turned into a commercial area. We passed a yarn shop, a paint while you drink wine store, and a pottery studio.

"As a rule, I try not to lie unless it's absolutely necessary, like softening the blow of bad news. If the news is sufficiently terrible, there is no need to make it worse."

"Being a Healer must be terribly sad at times."

The corners of his mouth turned down. "It can be, but I'm able to help the greater majority of patients." His smile returned.

The smell of savory meat and spicy sauce drifted through the air. My stomach growled. "Where is that delicious smell coming from?" I didn't see a sign for a restaurant.

"Just up ahead," he said. "It's a casual outdoor restaurant with a twist. I can't wait to see your reaction."

I poked him in the ribs. "Here I thought you were all kind and trustworthy."

"I am." He grabbed my hand and held it, which made my insides flutter. "I also like to see your face when you learn something new and fantastical. It's not much farther."

My mouth watered at the smell of meat roasting on a barbecue grill. We turned down a driveway. There was a wooden privacy fence that kept people from seeing into the back yard. When we came to the gate which was propped open, I stopped walking. My heart pounded with a mix of awe and disbelief. Dragons. Real live, slightly larger than elephant type dragons with bright red scales, blasted flames at a side of beef on a spit over an enormous barbecue grill.

"Dragons," I said, stating the obvious.

"We have a new patron," a dragon said, right before he blasted the meat again. The wave of heat almost had me stumbling back a step.

Bram tugged on my hand. "Come on. I'll introduce you."

Sure. I was about to be introduced to a dragon. I let Bram lead me toward the actual fire-breathing dragon doing my best not to appear freaked out.

"Ian Dent, this is Belinda Harbinger."

"Nice to meet you," the dragon said.

"I...nice to meet you, too."

Ian laughed. "Not used to talking dragons, are you?"

"I've only recently adjusted to talking cats," I admitted. "Dragons might take longer. Your barbecue smells wonderful."

"It's the searing," Ian said. "No flame can compete with the heat we use. Grab a seat. Someone will take your order."

"Thank you." I turned and let Bram led me to a picnic table under the shade of a majestic oak tree.

His grin was huge. "It's fun to see what I take for granted through new eyes."

"How could you ever take a dragon for granted?"

"Good question." An auburn haired woman with bright blue eyes approached us carrying a small notepad and a pen.

"Hello, Elise," Bram said. "I would never take you for granted. I'm aware of your presence while Belinda was not."

Elise tilted her head at him. "Nice recovery." She tapped her pen on the notepad. "Today we have brisket, ribs, or burgers served with corn on the cob and green beans."

"I'll have the brisket."

"Same for me," Bram said. "And two large sweet teas."

Elise returned a few moments later. Each plate held what looked like a pound of brisket covered in barbecue sauce that smelled divine.

I took a bite. The barbecue was tender and spicy and awesome. "This is amazing. I'm surprised Sadie or Dave hasn't mentioned it."

Bram wiped his mouth and leaned in. "Most Familiars stay away from dragons based on pure animal instinct."

That made a strange sort of sense.

When I finished eating my plate was still covered with food. "I need a carry out box."

Elise came back with a box before I could even ask. "I knew you'd need this." She pointed at Bram's plate. "I knew you wouldn't."

"I have a normal appetite for a fairy," Bram said. "You know flying burns extra calories."

"You go flying?" I asked.

Elise sized me up. "You must be new around here."

This female dragon seemed like a lay it all out on the table kind of person. "I've had some memory issues. I rediscovered Mystic Hills this summer."

"Wow." She leaned against the table. "Then you have so many things to learn. This one," she pointed at Bram. "Flies every morning. Sometimes our paths cross. The first time we met I almost blasted him out of the sky."

"If you flew faster," Bram said. "I might not have startled you."

Elise shook her head. "One of these days, Bram..."

"Stop flirting with the customers," Ian hollered from the grill. "People want to eat."

"Fine." She stood and sauntered away from the table.

Had she been flirting with Bram? Had Bram been flirting with me? He'd held my hand. That should mean something. Time to diffuse this awkwardness. I leaned closer to him. "Can fairies fly faster than dragons?"

"We'll never know," he said. "Because Ian would barbecue me if I went flying with Elise."

I tilted my head and studied him. "Was she flirting with you?"

He cleaned up his side of the table. "I'm never sure, and I have no intention of finding out."

In imitation of him, I cleaned up my side of the table and followed him to a trash can to throw away our debris. I stacked my books on top of my carry out box.

As we left the restaurant, I said, "Can I ask you questions about flying?" I wasn't sure what was appropriate.

"Of course."

"How often do you fly around town as opposed to walking?"

"I fly every morning for exercise. I also fly within my neighborhood as do most fairies. I portal mostly for my work but walk on Main Street."

"Why don't you fly everywhere?" If I had wings, I probably would.

"Like I mentioned to Elise, it burns a lot of calories. If I flew to all of my appointments for work, I'd need to eat six times a day instead of three."

I'd love to be able to eat six meals a day. And of course I'd want to fly, but given a choice eating whatever I wanted without putting on weight would be a dream come true.

When we reached Bram's office, he said, "I'm glad I ran into you. This was nice."

"It was." A gentle warmth spread through my body. A sense of well being, and anticipation.

He stood close enough where if he wanted to lean down and kiss me he could. Apparently he didn't want to because he turned and walked up the sidewalk to his office.

Slightly disappointed, I headed for my car while I replayed my latest activity with Bram. He'd held my hand, which you didn't normally do unless you were family, or you cared for someone romantically. Then again, maybe fairies held hand with friends. I didn't know. There had to be someone I could ask.

CHAPTER 13

I was not a thirteen year old girl so I would not focus on datable men and their behavior. If it was meant to be, it was meant to be. That was what I told myself as I sat on the rooftop terrace of the house that evening. Given the day I'd had, which by all accounts had gone rather well despite making no progress on figuring who had started this double trouble, I had fixed myself a bowl of cookies and cream ice-cream. It was creamy, crunchy, sweet goodness in a bowl. As I shoveled the frozen confection into my mouth, I watched the lights in the houses and the town below.

One side effect of Mystic Hills being situated above a bunch of ley lines was the evening lights, which looked a lot like the aurora borealis. Streaks of shimmering green and purple lit up the night sky. It was amazing. I remember Reed telling me that up here you didn't see all the manipulative plays for power and petty back stabbing that went on in Mystic Hills, you only saw the beauty.

"Belinda," Sadie's voice came from down below.

"On the roof," I yelled so she could find me.

I heard footsteps on the stairs which meant she was now in human form. When Sadie was in cat form, I rarely heard her coming.

"I wondered where you'd gotten to." She climbed onto the terrace and joined me at the small table.

"It's beautiful up here," I said.

"It's a shame that I hardly notice it anymore. For me, it's just normal."

I snorted. "Is anything in Mystic Hills ever normal?"

"That depends on how you define the term." She leaned toward me and sniffed. "Why do you smell of dragons?"

"I do?" I'd brushed my teeth earlier and flossed. "I had lunch at a barbecue place run by dragons."

"By yourself?" She sounded fearful.

"No. I went to a bookstore by Bram's office, and we went to lunch together."

"Oh." She leaned closer sporting a sly smile. "Was it a date?"

"That is a good question." I described how the lunch date happened and how he'd held my hand.

"Hand holding is a good sign," she said in a sing song voice.

"I wasn't sure if fairies held hands often or if it meant something."

"It had to have meant something," she said. "It's not like you're an old lady and he was giving you a hand to help you across a busy street."

"I hope you're right." The idea of dating Bram made my stomach wiggle around, or maybe that was the ice cream.

"Only time will tell," Sadie said. "Males, no matter the species, often don't know what they want."

"My ex wanted a very flexible yoga instructor," I said.

Sadie laughed. "Oh dear. I'd say that's a shame, but you're probably better off without him."

"You and Dave seem happy." I finished off the last bite of my ice cream.

"We are," Sadie said. "At first I was jealous of Celia, but she's totally into Orville."

"I wondered about that." I wasn't sure how to ask the next question. "Do sprites and people date?"

"I don't see why not," she said. "I'm not sure what the gossip circuit would make of it, but if they care for one another, I don't see how it could be wrong."

That seemed like an overly simplified view of the situation given the size difference. "I asked Bram about fairy genetics. Apparently wings trumps flightless genes every time."

"Are you picturing yourself holding a little winged baby?" she asked.

The question caught me off guard. It took a moment to formulate an answer. "No. I mean.... if, and let me preface this by saying I don't know if he even sees me as anything but a friend, but if we dated and one thing led to another and we ended up married with winged children, then does that mean I could never take them outside of Mystic Hills?"

"There are glamours to hide wings, but every time someone with non-human characteristics leaves Mystic Hills they are at risk for discovery."

"Have you traveled in the outside world?" I asked.

"No. I can pass as human. If I ever wanted to travel, it wouldn't be a problem, but I'm quite happy here. This is home."

Was it my home? Sometimes it felt like I belonged. Other times it felt like an interesting place for summer vacation. I still had months to decide, but in the back of my head I felt a clock ticking down.

I was engrossed in my werewolf book the next afternoon when a ghost whooshed into the living rom. He did not appear surprised. A broad smile lit his face and then he spotted me on the couch. "Excuse me, I think I died."

I set my book aside and nodded. "I believe you did. What's your name?"

"Thomas Wood."

"Is there anyone you'd like me to contact for you? Or are you ready to cross over?"

"I've been ready to go for a long time," he said. "I'm ready to see my Esther again."

Most of the ghosts I encountered were confused and struggling to come to terms with their untimely death, but Thomas was ready to move on to the next plane. If that was true, why did he need me? "I have a friend who can help you cross over."

"I can see the light," he said. "I wanted to tell someone where to find my body."

"Okay."

"I was sitting on a bench at the park on South Street feeding the birds." He poofed out of existence.

Hopefully he'd have a wonderful reunion with Esther. I pulled out my phone and dialed the police department. The officer I spoke to took down the information about Thomas like it wasn't a big deal. This time I guess it wasn't since Thomas more than likely died of old age and was happy to move on.

Twenty minutes later my reading was interrupted by a knock on the kitchen door. I opened it to find Mayor Castor and a police officer standing there, both wearing sour expressions.

"What can I do for you?"

The mayor entered without waiting for an invitation. The officer followed him inside and slammed the door.

Before I could ask what was going on, the mayor said, "Why didn't you tell us he'd been drained?"

"What are you talking about?" I backed up a few steps and put the kitchen table between us.

"Thomas Wood," the officer bit out. "He was drained and left for dead."

"And thanks to you and your aunt's interference, that is a crime," the mayor stated like I'd done something outrageous.

Anger pulsed through my body. "That man appeared to me and said he was happy to move on so he could be with his wife. He never even hinted that he'd been attacked let alone drained."

"That seems highly unlikely." The police officer sniffed like he smelled something rotten.

"This," I pointed back and forth between the two of them. "is bull hockey. A ghost appeared to me, and I reported the facts he shared. How was I supposed to know he'd been drained? I can see ghosts and hear them, but I can't read their minds."

Sadie padded into the room and hopped up on the table.

Celia buzzed in a moment later and landed next to the cat. "While I'm not sure what this bull hockey is Belinda referred to," the sprite said. "You are focusing your anger in the wrong direction. Perhaps you should focus on finding the person who committed the crime rather than berating the honest citizen who reported it."

"Scat," the police officer waved his hands at Sadie and possibly Celia. Sadie's orange fur puffed up making her appear twice her normal size, but she stayed right where she was.

Celia buzzed up in front of the officer's face. "You're lucky I don't offend easily. Otherwise, I might make every piece of fruit that enters your house rot and mold within minutes."

"Now, now." The mayor held his hands out like he was trying to calm the room. "I believe we may have gotten off on the wrong foot with this conversation. Belinda, I should have known you would have reported any insidious deaths. I believe the officer was appalled at what he found when he went to retrieve what he thought would be a citizen who passed away from natural causes."

If the mayor wanted to make nice, I'd play along. "I'm sure discovering he was the victim of foul play was disturbing." I couldn't wrap my head around why he hadn't told me he'd been attacked. "Do you think someone tricked him or used a spell, so he didn't know what happened?" I hoped it wasn't painful.

"I saw the body," the mayor said. "While the scene was unsettling, the man's face was relaxed. Hopefully he just drifted away."

"I could try to summon his spirit," I said. "But I've never called someone immediately after they crossed over." And I didn't want to interrupt his reunion.

The police officer shuffled his feet. "Let the man be. We'll start an investigation, and if we need to speak to him, I'll be in touch."

The two men left in the same abrupt manner in which they came. Once the door was closed, I plopped down in the kitchen chair. "Thanks for the backup."

"You have no idea how hard it is for me to remember not to yell at idiots who don't know I'm a Familiar," Sadie said.

"I'm happy to help," Celia said. "Some people always look to assign blame. I don't care for those people."

"Me either," I said. "I can't believe Thomas didn't tell me he'd been drained."

"Maybe he was so happy to be reunited with his family that he didn't mind," Sadie said.

My relaxed happy mood was gone.

"No use moping about things we can't control. We should invite people over for dinner," Sadie said.

"Why would we do that?"

"You can go back to your book if you like, but I thought having friends over for dinner might remind you why Mystic Hills is a good place."

Bad things happened in good places. I knew that, but Mystic Hills seemed to have more than its share of evil. Still Sadie was right. Who should we invite? Wait a minute. "We should invite our friends that have been split in two. Maybe if we put our heads together we can come up with a plan."

Getting both halves of Lisa and Nathan to attend had been a struggle. In the end they agreed to come if *Tea & Spirits* supplied the alcohol.

And that was how I ended up sitting at the magically extended kitchen table with the Grumpy Reed, Happy Reed, Serious Lisa, Relaxed Lisa, Workaholic Nathan, and Non-workaholic Nathan, Sadie, Dave, Victor, and Jezelle.

I'd ordered barbecue from the Dragons, made a salad, and purchased an assortment of cupcakes from *The Bakers Dozen*. Jezelle and both Reeds had brought the ingredients to make margaritas and an assortment of beer.

"This was a good idea," Dave said. "I can't remember the last time we all sat down together."

Victor passed him a margarita. "It is nice. We should do this once a month."

"Good idea," both Reeds said, in unison.

I laughed. "Sorry, that gets me every time." I pointed at the other twins. "Do you do that?"

"No," Relaxed Lisa said. "I think the Reed twins are closer than the rest of us."

Serious Lisa poured Italian dressing on her salad. "We don't spend much time together. That might be why."

Workaholic Nathan pointed at Sadie. "You're a Familiar?"

"Yes," she said. "My former witch kept me a secret, but after all this time I'm tired of hiding my true identity."

"But you're not telling anyone who your witch is," he said.

"No," Sadie glanced around. "Where's Celia?"

"I invited her and suggested she bring Orville, but she said they'd rather have a quiet dinner together."

"I can't stop going to his store," Relaxed Lisa said. "He has so many interesting things."

"I don't like that place," Jezelle said. "Something about it is...off. Where did all the stuff come from? I get the odd feeling that one day when I walk in there I'll see the bracelet I lost in high school or my grandmother's vase that's been missing for years."

That made me wonder. "Is there a spell to collect items that other people have given up looking for?"

"Oh, stop it," Relaxed Lisa said. "It's a thrift store with cool things. If you saw your grandma's vase in there it's because everyone's grandma had the same vase and one of them ended up in his store."

"You're probably right," I said just to move the conversation along. Maybe I'd ask Agatha or Yelena about that sort of spell.

"Why isn't Bram here?" Jezelle asked, giving me a pointed look.

"I invited him, but he had other plans." I said this in a factual manner like it wasn't a big deal. I was still trying to decipher our lunch date or non-date.

"Don't give up on him," Jezelle said. "He's brilliant but a bit oblivious when it comes to women. It took his wife six months to convince him they should get engaged."

I set my forkful of barbecue down with a thunk, my appetite suddenly gone. "He's married?"

"Widowed," Jezelle rushed to clarify. "Sorry, I thought he would have told you."

A wave of embarrassment washed over me. My cheeks burned. It felt like she had set me up. "Excuse me." I pushed away from the table and stalked into the living room. When we talked about her relationship with Reed, she told me no one had irreparably broken Bram's heart. How could she leave out such a crucial piece of information?

Jezelle crept into the living room moving slowly. "I'm sorry. I really thought you knew."

I let loose with the rant that was currently playing on a loop in my head. "You told me he'd never had a severely broken heart. I'm pretty sure being widowed would cause some significant damage."

"That is true," she said. "But they were separated when she died. He grieved her, but it wasn't like he lost a woman he was madly in love with."

That did make it a little better. "You still should have told me."

"You're right." She put her hand on my shoulder. "I'm sorry. Can you come back to dinner?"

I nodded. She gave me a quick hug, and we went back into the kitchen. Conversation paused as we entered the room and then it started back up again.

After downing half of a margarita, I decided everything was fine.

When it was time for dessert, Relaxed Lisa said, "Nathan and I have an announcement."

"Oh, crap," Serious Lisa muttered.

"We're moving in together," Relaxed Lisa said as she bounced in her chair.

"That's great," I chimed in. Sadie, Dave, and Victor added congratulations.

Workaholic Nathan said, "I feel I should have been consulted."

"You sleep at the office most nights," Non-workaholic Nathan shrugged.

"I'm sure I'll regret this," Serious Lisa said. "Nathan with a work ethic, if you need a place to stay to get away from them." She gestured at the other Reed and Lisa. "You can use our guest bedroom."

Workaholic Nathan nodded at her. "Thank you for the offer. I'll keep that in mind."

Sadie set two platters of cupcakes in the center of the table. "We have chocolate, vanilla, and strawberry flavored cupcakes. And there's enough for everyone to have several, so eat up or you're taking some home."

I picked a chocolate cupcake with vanilla frosting, peeled off the wrapper, and took a bite. The icing tasted like whipped cream and the cake was dense and fudge-like. Yum. I took small bites in between sips of coffee, to make it last longer. I only needed one cupcake.

Sadie grabbed a vanilla cupcake and put it on my plate. "You have to try this. The icing is salted caramel."

Uh-oh. It was already on my plate, so I had to eat it. Darn it. Rationalization accomplished. I peeled off the wrapper and took a bite. It was as divine as the first one I ate. "These cupcakes are amazing."

"Grace knows her baked goods," Dave said. "She always has the best booth at Summer Solstice Festival. Do you know what game you're doing for *Tea & Spirits*?"

"We host a game?" I remember the mayor referring to something like that, but I hadn't thought about it.

"Last year we did tea pong, instead of beer pong," Jezelle said.

"People bounce ping pong balls into cups of tea?" I deduced.

"Yes. If they make it in the teacup they can have a free non-alcoholic drink," Jezelle said. "Unless you want to change things up and play a different game."

"If you have what you need for that game let's stick with it."

The rest of dessert was fairly uneventful. When everyone swore they couldn't eat another bite, we packed up extra cupcakes for people to take home.

Happy Reed came to speak to me. "Jezelle didn't mean to upset you earlier. We both thought Bram would have told you."

Maybe that was what bothered me the most. "He hasn't old me much about himself. Half the time I think he's interested and the other half I think we're just friends. It's confusing and I wish he'd pick a lane."

Reed laughed and pulled me into a quick hug. "It will all work out how it's meant to be."

His warmth surrounded me for a moment, and I relaxed into it. "Thanks."

He walked over to Jezelle and kissed her lightly on the lips. Just a peck, but there was real affection there. I was simultaneously happy for them and sad for myself.

CHAPTER 14

The next day, I decided to go return the library books I'd finished. They weren't due for another two weeks, but maybe I could find some information while I was there. A different librarian manned the front desk today. I handed her my books and introduced myself.

"Hello, I'm Belinda Harbinger."

She scanned my books before placing them on a cart. "Nice to meet you. I'm Jane Harris."

How could I start her talking? "Do you have any resources about games for the Summer Solstice Festival?"

"We do. Are you looking for new ideas for a game, or are you interested in the historical aspect?"

"Both," I said. "I own *Tea & Spirits,* and we plan to play tea pong again this year but I thought I'd see if there was anything else we might want to play in the bar."

"Come with me." She led me down an aisle with leather bound books. "You're not the first person to come to me about historical games. I pulled several books about magical party games for another patron not long ago."

My breath caught. Had someone researched the coin games, looking for a drinking game that altered people?

"Did they find what they needed?" I asked.

"Yes. They were specifically interested in drinking games. Let me see." She ran her fingertips along the titles of the books. "There was one book they kept out longer than the others, so I'm guessing they found it the most useful." She continued down the aisle. "Here it is." She pulled the book off the shelf and handed it to me. *Playful Party Games for Young and Old.*

I needed a little more information. "Thank you. Do you know who checked it out last so I don't accidentally end up planning the same game for *Tea & Spirits* that another business is already using?"

"I'm not supposed to share information, but I don't think he'd mind. Orville from Orville's Oddities checked out the book. Now that I think about it, I believe he was researching a game someone brought into the store. Our other librarian finds the best cardigans there, but I never find any clothes. I do have a lovely collection of earrings thanks to his store." She brushed aside her dark blond hair to reveal stunning blue topaz earrings.

"Those are beautiful," I said.

"Thank you. I used to worry about wearing jewelry that was too dressy for the library. Then I realized people rarely see them due to my hair. They are more for me than anyone else, and if they make me happy then why shouldn't I wear them?"

"That's a good attitude to have."

"Look at me being chatty."

"You've been very helpful," I said. "Thank you."

After checking the book out, I headed to one of the study tables on the second floor. A library was one of the few places you could read a book and completely avoid conversation. I'd started reading at the library because my ex always interrupted me when I was deep into a story. On one occasion when I asked him not to interrupt me again, he'd replied with, "What, it's not like you're doing anything. You're just reading."

I should have broken up with him then and there. In retrospect, the flexible yoga instructor had done me a favor.

Seated at a table with a woman copying recipes from a cookbook, I flipped through the my book until I came to a section about games with coins. The book posted a clear warning that these games could alter people's personalities or damage relationships. What the heck?

The first game featured a coin which matched people romantically. That would certainly end some relationships. What person in their right mind would agree to play? The next few games included coins that turned people into animals. Nope. Not playing those games.

Then I found it. The game that promised to set the players free from their worries and responsibilities. The happy and mad faced coin in the photo matched the one I'd given Bram. The rules of the game were clearly delineated along with the possible consequences. Had Orville researched the game and then given it to two witches to bring into *Tea & Spirits*? Why would he do that? Without a motive it didn't make sense.

The wooden chair beside me scraped across the library floor as it was pulled out. I didn't turn to see who it was because library etiquette differed from most social situations. The lady with the cookbook gathered up her things and left. The silence in the room hung heavy, and there was no sound of pages flipping or a book sliding across the table like normal. What was the person doing? I caved and turned to see who sat beside me and had to fight to keep surprise off my face.

Mrs. Fairbanks sat there studying me. "What are you reading, dear? And you should know I can spot a lie a mile away."

A sense of dread swamped me. Why was I the object of this power crazed woman's attention. And how could I make her go away?

I slid my arm away from the book, so she could see I wasn't trying to hide anything and worded my response carefully. "Jezelle said we play tea pong for the Summer Solstice Festival. I thought I'd look for some fun alternatives."

"Drinking games are low class. They encourage irresponsible behavior and excessive drinking. If you'd banned them from your establishment, we wouldn't have these strange twins running around town."

Was she trying to provoke me? I wouldn't give her the satisfaction, but I also wasn't going to act like a doormat. "I wasn't there the evening your ex-daughter-in-law played that game. You'd think the box would have come with a warning." I opened the book to the chapter about the coin games and pushed it toward her. "They were thoughtful enough to forewarn people in the book. It's almost like the people who brought the game into *Tea & Spirits* wanted to cause chaos. Isn't that strange? What could anyone gain from splitting random citizens? Unless it wasn't random." I waited to see if she'd give anything away.

"Maybe it was, maybe it wasn't. There are all sorts of games that people, especially people without any real magic, should avoid playing." She leaned back in her chair and studied me like I was some sort of lower life form. "Don't you agree?"

That sounded vaguely threatening. Doing my best to appear undisturbed by her presence, I said, "I've never been interested in games that manipulate people. I prefer puzzles. The rules are clear and if you figure it out everything comes together and gives you a clear picture."

"The library rents puzzles. Were you aware of that?"

"I was not. Thanks for telling me. I'll have to check them out."

"Was that a joke?" she asked.

I ran my last statement through my head and smiled. "Sorry, unintentional pun."

"If you're ever interested in selling your aunt's house, keep me in mind." She pulled a business card from her jacket pocket and set it on the open book.

"I have no plans to sell, but if I ever change my mind, I'll let you know."

"Have a nice day, dear." She gave me a thousand watt smile and then pushed her chair back and stood in one smooth motion.

"You too," I said as she turned and walked away.

Given the crazy power-hungry vibe that woman put off, there was no way I was touching her business card. It looked wrong. Most realtor cards I'd seen had the agent's picture on them. This one was black with a house sketched on it in blood red. No name, no address for their business, just the odd crimson house.

I closed the book, leaving the disturbing card sticking out. Maybe I was paranoid, but Mrs. Fairbanks and her creepy business card were giving me really bad vibes. I picked up the book and took it down to the front desk where Jane sat checking in books.

"This is going to sound crazy, but a witch who frightens me put a business card in this book, and for some reason I don't want to touch it."

Jane frowned. "We have a spell to detect books that contain hexes or books that have been cursed. Who gave you the card?"

Time to hedge my bets. "I hope she's not a friend of yours. She may be perfectly nice, but she's so intimidating. It was Mrs. Fairbanks."

Her eyebrows shot up. "She is a scary one. Let me see what spells we have on hand." In the top drawer she opened, I spotted several vials of pre-made spells. Jane grabbed one. "This should do it." She pulled out the stopper and said, "Detect a curse or hex on this book before a patron takes a look."

The purple powder shot out of the vial, it swirled and enveloped the book. Nothing happened.

"You're all good. If there was a hex the powder would have flashed red."

"Thanks for checking, I—"

Hot air hit my face at the same time I heard a crackle and then a boom. Flames shot up from the desk. I stumbled backwards and fought to regain my balance.

Jane screamed in outrage and then grabbed a vial from the drawer which she dumped onto the book. "Fire out, beyond a doubt."

The flames gradually lowered leaving behind the charred remnants of the book and drifting ash.

I stood frozen, anger roaring through my body like a freight train. "What the—"

"What happened?" Mrs. Kingsley came running.

Jane slumped against the desk. Soot blackened her face and hands. She made eye contact with me. "Someone used a business card as a bookmark. For some reason it caught fire."

"That's terrible." Mrs. Kingsley glanced back and forth between the two of us. "Are you both all right? Should I call a Healer?"

"No. I'm just...angry." There that was honest.

Jane smacked her hand on the desk. "Me too. I'm furious. Who thought this would be a funny joke? Fire in a library is never funny."

Since Jane hadn't named Mrs. Fairbanks as the person who placed the card, I wasn't going to mention it either. At least not to anyone at the library.

"You two should go clean up," Mrs. Kingsley said. "Use the restroom in the lounge so you'll have a little privacy."

I followed Jane to a side door and down a dimly lit hallway to a room with a view of the parking lot. She walked past the lunch tables and the refrigerator which hummed quietly in the corner. When we reached our destination, and I caught sight of myself in the bathroom mirror, I gasped.

Soot covered my face and coated the front of my shirt. And my hair...it looked like I had a horrid case of blackened dandruff. I wasn't sure where to even begin. Maybe I should go home and take a shower.

Jane grabbed a paper towel and wet it. Wiping her face turned the soot into something resembling black paint. "I think we need magic to clean up this mess." She walked back out to the lounge and returned with a vial of powder. "This should clean us and the bathroom. Keep your eyes closed until it's done. It won't damage your eyes, but it does sting."

I clamped my eyes and mouth shut.

"Clean and restore so it's like before," Jane said.

I smelled a fresh clean scent and felt a breeze whoosh across my face and body, tugging at my hair. Once the sensation stopped, I opened my eyes to find the soot gone along with my mascara and powder.

"That's much better." Jane pulled a tube of lipstick from her pocket and reapplied it.

"Should I report this to the police?" I knew the standard belief about Fairbanks being untouchable.

"It's not worth the possible backlash. If anyone asks, tell them you left the book on the counter and walked away. We think it was a practical joke by one of our regular patrons that went a little too far."

"She tried to set me on fire," I bit out.

"The fire seemed to be contained to the book. We were caught in the fallout, but we weren't burned."

"So, book burning is a good thing?" I asked.

"No," she snapped, and then laughed. "In this case it might be. I think I'll go to Orville's on my lunch break. Hopefully I'll find something that makes me smile."

Jane had been kind and helpful and she didn't deserve this. "Sorry to drag you into my mess."

She gave a tight smile and left the room. I stood there at the sink trying to gather up my—what? Courage, fortitude, the will to go on.

CHAPTER 15

I slipped out of the library through a side door so I wouldn't have to deal with the mess at the front desk and anyone who might be asking questions about why a book had burst into flames. Maybe people would believe the explanation of a practical joke gone wrong. Perhaps the citizens of Mystic Hills had learned not to ask questions when a story sounded illogical because the truth was something they didn't want to know. My phone rang before I made it to my car. I stopped under a shade tree next to the sidewalk.

"Hello?"

"It's Sadie. What's wrong?"

"I'm fine," I said. "I'm coming home. I'll fill you in then."

All three of my housemates, in human form, waited for me at the kitchen table when I entered the house. Sadie's human hair seemed to be standing on end like her cat fur did when she was stressed.

"Sorry to worry you," I said.

"I'm glad you're not injured," Sadie said. "Sit and tell us what happened."

My throat felt dry. "Lilly, can I have a glass of ice water?"

My drink appeared on the table. I sat and drank half of it. "That's better." I recapped my trip to the library, what I learned, and how it ended with the crescendo of a book fire.

"That woman is a menace," Sadie said.

"It sounds like you stood up to her, which might be why she set your book on fire," Dave said. "She's used to people who tuck tail and run."

"It's not like I went after her," I pointed out. "I attempted to have an honest conversation."

"She probably isn't used to that," Victor said. "You should consider yourself lucky the fire was contained within the book."

"If that book had been in my car this day would have turned out differently. My car could have caught fire, or I could have wrecked. So, this may not have been as harmless as you think."

"That woman is far from harmless," Victor warned. "The blazing book was a sign of things to come if you don't stay away from her."

"I agree," Sadie said. "You need to avoid that woman at all costs."

"That was my plan all along." I threw my hands up in frustration. "She tracked me down at the library. I didn't go looking for trouble."

"You're a Harbinger," Victor said. "I'm pretty sure trouble finds you."

I shivered. "On that cheery note, I'm going to read in my room. I need a happily ever after because I've had enough reality for one day."

Celia portaled into my room while I was reading. "I want tea, but the cats are sleeping. Will you join me on the rooftop terrace?"

I was at a good part of my book, but Celia had been a great help during this weird ordeal. Flesh and blood friends had to trump fictional friends...sometimes. This was one of those times.

"I'd love to. We can go up and Lilly will transport the tea."

Celia clapped. "Thank you." She buzzed out of my bedroom door, and I followed. Her wings were much faster than my feet, and they gave her a more direct route to the roof. By the time I climbed up the back fire escape she'd already asked Lilly for tea and tiny lemon meringue cookies.

I'd planned to ask for a human sized cup and regular sized cookies, but Celia was excited about her dishes, so I sipped from a tiny cup, ate tiny cookies, and didn't complain.

"How are things going with you and Orville?" I asked.

She blushed. "Being away from him has made me realize how much I care for him."

"That's wonderful," I said.

"I'm not sure he feels the same way. He's always happy to see me, but then he starts making comments about the time and how it's late and he has things to do."

I thought of the lady in the bookstore and the advice she'd given me about Bram. "The only way to know how he feels about you for sure is to ask him."

Celia sipped her tea and then set the cup down. "Right now I have hope that he cares as deeply for me as I do for him. If I ask and discover he does not feel the same, then I lose hope and possibly my best friend."

That made a twisted sort of sense. "In this magical town you'd think someone would have worked out a spell to make dating and relationships easier."

"Love is its own sort of unique magic so it is mostly resistant to spells. You can't create love from nothing, but you can revive it or extinguish it."

"Revive or extinguish...those both sound kind of shady like you're doing something not quite right."

"For the most part people know not to mess with love spells. The results are not often what the witch intended." She ran her finger along the handle of her tea cup. "Some people have such profound cases of grief that they cast a spell to extinguish their love for the person who died unexpectedly, but those situations rarely ends well. Without the love which was such a big part of their life it's like the person is adrift and they aren't sure why. Love, even when it turns to grief is the anchor that holds all of us in our assigned spot. Without love we drift through life."

"I've never heard it described like that."

"Don't get me wrong," Celia said. "I'm not saying that without romantic love you're lost. There are many types of love: familial love, love of a pet, love between friends. If you have some sort of connection anchoring you in place then you can thrive."

I finished off my small cup of tea and poured another. "Would you like a refill?"

"No. And thank you for drinking out of my teacups. Sometimes the size difference is annoying."

I had questions about that. "You range in size from a firefly to a Barbie Doll. What determines how big you are?"

She laughed. "My need, I suppose. Some Sprites are as tall as trees and some the size of sesame seeds."

"Have you ever wondered how Orville would react if you were the size of a human female?"

Her mouth fell open and then she closed it. "Do you think that is the problem?"

"I don't know." I sipped my tea. "It's one variable."

"Lilly, can you transport my tea set to the Belinda's room?" she asked.

In answer, the tea set vanished.

"Come on." Celia buzzed down the stairs. I followed, assuming she was headed for my room.

When I walked through my bedroom door, Celia stood there, about five and a half feet tall, in front of the dresser mirror. Her skin was iridescent like her wings. Her blue hair brushed her shoulders, and her green eyes sparkled in delight. The pale blue dress accented her lithe figure. "Look at me. I could be a person." She spun in a circle.

Sadie and Dave trotted into the room.

"The scent of sprite exploded through the house," Dave said. "We were worried about you."

Celia sat on my bed, and the cats jumped up beside her. She stroked their heads "I'm fine, my furry friends. Just larger now. Maybe Orville will see me more clearly this way."

Both cats purred. Sadie moved away and shook her head. "Might I make one suggestion about your appearance?"

"Of course," Celia said.

Sadie shifted to her human form where she looked like a beautiful forty year old blond. "If possible you should age your face to make it look more adult, like mine."

Celia reached out and traced a fingertip along Sadie's laugh lines. "These are only for adults?"

"How old is Orville?" I asked.

"I have no idea," Celia said. "His hair has sparkled like silver for years."

"I think he has grown children," Sadie said. "So, he's at least in his fifties. If your face looked more like an adult it might make him see you as someone he could spend time with."

Celia huffed out a breath. "First I'm not big enough, and now I'm not adult enough?"

Uh-oh. I stood and put my hand on her shoulder. "We're just guessing. You are beautiful no matter what your size, and we know he enjoys spending time with you. If you want to know how he feels or doesn't feel and why, you'll have to ask him."

"Phooey." She spun in a circle and shrunk down to her normal Barbie size. "I don't want to ask. I'm afraid of the answer." She flew over to the tea set which Lilly had transferred to my dresser.

Time to redirect her. "Forget about him. Let's drink our tea and talk about what flowers you think I should plant in the flower beds in front of the house."

She buzzed with excitement. "I could plant them for you. Do you have a favorite flower?"

In truth I had given zero thought to this. I had just wanted to distract Celia from her man problems. Then it hit me. "Would it be cliche to plant lilies?"

Celia's wings vibrated so fast I couldn't see them. "That's a lovely idea."

"Lilly would you be okay with lilies in the yard?"

The lights blinked once which, meant no.

I was surprised. Lilly was normally so agreeable. "You'd rather have something besides lilies?"

The lights blinked twice.

"Is it because your name is Lilly, and it would be confusing?" Sadie asked.

The lights blinked twice again.

"That makes sense," I said. "Is there any way you can show me the flowers you'd like us to plant?"

A bouquet of yellow daffodils and purple irises appeared on my dresser.

"Those are pretty," I said.

"They are a lovely combination," Celia said. "I'll get started on the yard right away."

"My mother always plants daffodils." A weird pang of home sickness hit me. "Her back yard is full of them." When I was younger, I helped her plant flowers. Now she did the gardening, and I admired it in the evening when I visited.

"Why do you look sad?" Celia asked.

"Just thinking about my mom," I said.

"She should come back to Mystic Hills and stay with us," Celia said.

"She didn't receive the family gift," I explained. "She was encouraged to leave."

"I'm sorry," Celia said. "I didn't know."

"It all worked out. She met my father in college. They married and had me and life went on."

"But you're here now," Celia said. "And your parents are not."

Bam, another pang of homesickness hit. "True. I'm off work for the summer. I'll probably go home for the school year and then come back next summer."

"Have you decided that?" Sadie asked.

"No." I wiped at the tears in my eyes. "I haven't thought about it for a while, but I miss my parents."

"Like I said before," Sadie reminded me. "You can always come back one weekend a month during the school year to keep our bond strong."

"And you don't have to decide now. You have months to work out what you want," Dave said.

I sniffled. "Sorry about this. I don't know where this burst of emotion came from."

"Flowers can do that," Celia said. "We associate a certain flower with a certain person. Even if the person isn't here, the flower reminds us of our feelings."

"My mother loves sunflowers," Dave said. "Always grows them in her yard."

"What's your favorite flower, Celia?" Sprites seemed to have a special connection to plants.

"I love Lily of the Valley. Each tiny bloom is like a perfect bell, and they are sprite sized. Like sprites they create beauty but if they are attacked, they will fight back."

"What do you mean?" I asked.

"They are small and unassuming, but they are poisonous from their petals to their roots."

"I didn't know that." And the comparison to a sprite was kind of frightening.

"You were surprised when Mrs. Fairbanks backed down after I threatened to blacken her yard. It's because she knows sprites can be vicious if you threaten something we love. Speaking of love, and being brave, I'm going to see Orville." Blue sparkles filled the air and Celia was once again human sized. "Wish me luck."

"Good luck," I said. "If he acts startled stay and visit anyway. It might take him awhile to see you in a new light."

Celia opened a portal and zipped through it.

"There you all are," Victor said from my doorway. "I fell asleep in my room while I was reading and when I went downstairs I couldn't find anyone."

Dave hopped off the bed and shifted into his human form. "Sorry. Next time we'll slide a note under your door to let you know where you can find us."

"I sense your sarcasm, but that's not a bad idea." Victor left the room and Dave followed him.

Sadie hopped off the bed and padded into the hallway.

I picked up my phone and called my parents. The phone rang and rang. Huh. They must be out and about. Hopefully they were doing something fun rather than going to the grocery store. I left a voicemail which I was sure neither of them would check. At least it was proof I called. I needed to make more of an effort to reach out while I was away. My stomach growled. Had I eaten lunch? I checked the clock. It was quarter after two, and I hadn't eaten anything but sprite sized cookies since breakfast. Time for lunch.

I headed downstairs, but before I reached the living room a gray mass swirled in front of me.

"Oh, crud."

The swirling mist solidified into Mrs. Kingsley, the librarian. She studied my face and then frowned. "Not again."

"What happened?"

"I have no idea. I planned to go shopping." Her form blurred. "I know I left the house."

"Let me call Violet and your other half," I said.

"They're both at Violet's house," she said. "Meet me there."

Sadie stood at the bottom of the steps. "Who was it?"

I explained and then used the kitchen phone to call the police. I reported the death, and the fact that Mrs. Kingsley had not mentioned being drained.

"Any idea where she died?" the officer asked.

"No. Sorry."

Sadie rode with me to Violet's house.

"It's like the twins are being targeted," I said. "Can you call Reed and ask him and Jezelle to warn Nathan and Lisa?"

She pulled out her phone and made the call.

When we pulled into the driveway, Violet and her other mother, Mrs. Kingsley, sat in Adirondack chairs on the front porch.

I climbed out of the car. "We need to go inside. Now."

Mrs. Kingsley frowned. "What's wrong?"

Once we were inside with the door locked, I touched the librarian's arm. "Your other half's ghost came to me."

"There you are," Ghost Mrs. Kingsley flew into the room with Ghost Violet by her side.

"Do remember what happened?" I asked.

Her gray form shifted, becoming larger. "I left my house, and that's it."

"She was supposed to run errands and then come over for dinner later tonight," Violet said.

I had a bad feeling about this.

"You suspect she was drained like me?" Ghost Violet said.

I nodded.

"What now? Do we wait for the police to call?" Mrs. Kingsley asked.

"I don't like it." Violet crossed her arms over her chest. "But I think that's all we can do."

"You could go to Yelena," Sadie suggested. "She might have a spell which allows a ghost to find their body."

"Really?"

"Do you really believe this is the first time a body has gone missing in Mystic Hills?" Sadie asked.

"What about the police?" Violet suggested. "Shouldn't they use that sort of spell?"

"They should," Sadie said.

Violet's house phone rang, startling all of us. She ran into the kitchen to answer it. Her side of the conversation consisted of yes and no responses. After hanging up, she came back into the living room and sat on the couch. She blinked, and a tear ran down her face. "They found the body. It was drained and left over at South Street Park."

"It's okay," Mrs. Kingsley moved closer to her daughter and pulled her into a hug. "I'm still here and once this is over, my other half and I will recombine, just like you and Violet."

"I know." Violet sniffled. "It's so awful. Why is this happening?"

"It's probably happening because someone knows they won't be charged for draining one of each twin," I said.

"It might be selfish," Ghost Violet said to the ghost of her mother, "But I'm glad you're here. I've been so lonely."

"I'm glad to be with you, too," Ghost Mrs. Kingsley said.

"Did you warn the other twins?" Violet asked.

"Yes," I said. "I wish we could do more."

"Figure out how to recombine us," Mrs. Kingsley said. "Then hopefully this nightmare will end."

Once we were back in the car, I sat with the engine running.

"Is something wrong?" Sadie asked. "Besides the obvious."

"I don't know what to do." I squeezed the steering wheel in frustration. "I swear Mrs. Fairbanks is behind all of this, but I don't have any proof. Even if I did, I'm not sure anyone would care." I rubbed my temples. "It's maddening." This was when leaving Mystic Hills seemed like a really good idea. But I couldn't abandon my friends.

"Let's go see Yelena," Sadie said. "I think it's time we figure out how to protect ourselves and our friends."

Yelena sat on a stool behind the counter, reading a book when we walked into her store. I recognized the werewolf on the cover. "I just finished that book. It was amazing."

"No spoilers." Yelena held up a finger in warning.

"Of course not. After you finish it, we should get together and talk about it."

Yelena inserted a bookmark and then set the book down and smiled. "I'd like that. Now how can I help you today?" She glanced at Sadie. "I'm sorry. Have we met?"

"In my cat form. My name is Sadie. I'm a Familiar."

"Nice to meet you on two feet, Sadie. Were you looking for anything in particular?"

Sadie moved closer. "Do you have any Daggers of Life?"

Yelena's eyebrows came together. "Why would you need one of those?"

"What is it?" I asked.

"A Dagger of Life collects blood from the person who is stabbed. It's kind of an oxymoron," Yelena said. "The person dies while the dagger collects their lifeblood."

I had an idea of where Sadie was going with this. I wasn't sure I approved, but drastic times called for extreme measures.

"Someone is draining one of each twin," I said. "They've killed two so far."

"Because it's not against the law since half the person is still alive," Yelena guessed.

"Do you have the daggers?" Sadie asked. "If we could give one to each twin, they might be able to defend themselves."

Yelena walked over to a cabinet and opened the bottom drawer. She pulled out a tray of knives and set it aside. She pulled out another smaller tray that had been hidden underneath and set it on the counter.

Light glinted off the silver blades of what appeared to be pocket knives. Each had an elaborate handle carved from something off white. The hair on my arms stood up. "Is that bone?"

"Yes," Yelena said. "It's a component of the spell."

Of course it was.

"You must understand," Yelena said. "These are deadly weapons. If you stab a person with this knife, and leave the blade in their body, it will drain them. If you pull the blade out, the collection process stops."

"So, you can use them without killing someone." Because killing someone, no matter how evil they were, was not on my agenda.

"Yes," she said. "It only takes five minutes to drain a person. If you use them, be mindful to remove the blade after a few minutes."

"We'll take ten," Sadie said. "I'd like them wrapped individually."

We delivered our strange and slightly scary gifts to the remaining twins. None of them questioned whether they were necessary. By the time we were back at the house I craved comfort carbs.

Sadie, Dave, Victor, and I sat around the kitchen table eating toasted cheese sandwiches with tomato soup.

"Such a simple sandwich," Victor said. "But it's one of my favorites."

"It's bread, butter, and cheese," Dave said. "What's not to love?"

I ignored my soup in favor of a second sandwich. "My mother used to put crispy bacon inside with the cheese."

"Oh," Dave said. "That is almost obscene."

"She's an amazing cook."

"Have you called your parents lately?" Victor asked.

"I tried earlier today, but they didn't answer."

CHAPTER 16

The next morning, Reed sat in the kitchen drinking coffee when I came downstairs for breakfast. I'd already showered and dressed, which was good because he'd seen me with bedhead quite a few times.

"Good morning," I said.

He grunted a response and drank his coffee.

Uh-oh. Was this Grumpy?

"Before you ask, I'm not him," he said.

I poured my own cup of coffee and went to the refrigerator for creamer. "Him who?"

"The nice guy. No need to make small talk. I'm waiting for my dad."

I added creamer to my coffee. How should I respond to his rude announcement? "Does that mean you'd prefer I not talk to you?"

"Yes."

Okay then. "Lilly, can I have a bowl of granola cereal with strawberries and banana?"

The cereal appeared on the table across from Grumpy. I considered picking it up and going to eat someplace else, but I wasn't about to let this Reed run me out of my own kitchen.

My brain threw out all sorts of question...things I wanted to ask him, but he'd set the ground rules, and I didn't want to deal with his negativity, so I sat and ate.

After a few minutes, he said, "Huh, I didn't think that would work."

"What?" I asked.

"Telling you I didn't want to talk. You're normally so chatty."

"You're normally cranky," I shot back, "so I figured staying mute was my best option."

He narrowed his eyes.

I pointed a finger at him. "Don't even think about it. I kept quiet. You started this conversation."

"My mistake." He sipped his French roast.

If he'd stayed silent, I wouldn't be annoyed right now. He hadn't wanted small talk. I could work around that stipulation. "Have you and Jezelle figured out anything about who might have brought the game into *Tea & Spirits?*"

"No." He rapped his knuckles on the table. "Have you had any luck?"

"There seems to be a common cast of suspects. Mrs. Fairbanks has been at Orville's, and she's connected to Violet who is one of the twins. Lisa, also a twin, approved a large payment of blood between Mrs. Fairbanks and Orville."

"So, you think Orville or Mrs. Fairbanks could have started all of this?"

"Her, rather than him," I said. "He's happy in his own world. She seems like a wicked witch plotting to take over the universe."

He nodded. "She is power hungry and for the most part untouchable."

"Great."

"You need to remember something. You don't have to stay in Mystic Hills." He placed his hand on top of mine. "You have a way out."

His touch was warm even if his words weren't.

"Is this your way of telling me you'd wish I'd go home so you could forget about me?"

He ran his fingertips from my hand up my forearm and back down again. "That's the problem, Belinda. I could never forget about you which is ironic since your forgot all about me."

He didn't sound angry anymore, just sad. Tears filled my eyes. There was so much I wanted to say, but my throat tightened. "If I could go back and change that day, I'd refuse my mom's ultimatum, I wouldn't let her remove my memories, and I'd stay here with you."

Warmth flowed between us. He sighed and pulled his hand away, taking the comforting heat with him. "If I could change anything, I never would have kissed you in the first place."

I closed my eyes tight, but the tears came anyway. I swallowed over the lump in my throat.

"I'm not saying that to hurt you," he said. "Mystic Hills is deadly. I'd rather you be happy and safe someplace else."

"Knowing about you and Mystic Hills makes it hard to go back to my old life."

He picked up his coffee spoon and tapped it on the table. "And Bram?"

"We're getting to know each other," I said. "I'm not sure what will happen." Since we were being honest, I stared straight at him and held his gaze. "He wouldn't be my first choice."

His eyes darkened. "We can't always have what we want."

"Do you love Jezelle?" I blurted out.

"We're good together," he said. "She's my best friend. She's loyal. I know she'll never leave me. And that's good enough."

Was it though? My heart ached for him, for Jezelle, and for me. There was nothing left to be said, so I finished my cereal, stood, then took my dishes to the sink.

Victor walked into the kitchen and must have read the room. "Everything okay?"

"Everything is fine," Reed said. "We hashed out a few things. Right, Belinda?"

I stayed facing the sink and refilled my coffee so Victor couldn't see I'd been crying. "We're good."

Reed walked to the door. Out of the corner of my eye, I saw him pause with his hand on the doorknob. Then he shoved it open and marched out. Victor stopped at the door. "Are you okay?"

I sighed. "I will be."

He left, too. I sat back down at the kitchen table. Should I have bared my heart to this version of Reed? He was the one I'd hurt by not coming back. Then there was Jezelle. She'd flat out told me she knew he didn't love her. She deserved better, but since she was aware of where she stood, I had no business interfering. I needed to forget my feelings for Reed, just put them away in a box somewhere and let them gather dust.

I sat in the living room reading when something gray whooshed into the room and swirled in front of me. It solidified into Nathan. "Save Lisa," he gasped.

Holy crap. "Where is she?"

"My house." He faded away.

My hands shook as I pulled out my phone and dialed Bram.

Thankfully he answered. "It's Belinda. Nathan's ghost told me I need to help Lisa. I think they're at his house."

"Where are you?"

"Home. In the living room. Can you portal here and take me there? Please."

In answer, a portal swirled open in front of the fireplace. I ran through it to Bram's office. Bram grabbed his bag of potions in one hand and wrapped his other arm around me. "Hold on."

Another portal opened, and my heart beat double time as we stepped through to Nathan's front porch.

He pulled several blue bottles out of the bag he carried. "These are anesthesia potions. Normally you drink them, but they can be absorbed through the skin. If someone comes toward you splash them with the potion. It will slow them down."

Bad idea. I did not want to rely on my ability to hit a moving target with liquid. "I'll go for Lisa, and you can distract the bad guy, whoever it is."

"Okay. Ready?" Bram asked.

I nodded.

He opened the portal into Nathan's living room. My breath caught at the grim scene. Nathan lay sprawled across the couch with his eyes open, staring at the empty fireplace.

"Get away from me," Lisa screamed from somewhere.

Holy crap. We dashed through the portal. Heart pounding, I grabbed a poker from the fireplace and handed one to Bram.

"This won't kill you," a woman's voice snapped. "Stop running away from me."

We snuck into the kitchen and saw Amber, the woman who'd broken up Violet's marriage, on one side of the kitchen table holding a silver dagger. Lisa stood on the other side, holding her dagger of life.

Bram unstoppered his bottle of anesthesia potion and splashed it at the back of Amber's head.

"What the—?" She whipped around and charged Bram with the knife. I swung the metal poker like a baseball bat, aiming at her head. She blocked the blow with her arm, but howled in pain.

Bram threw a second bottle of potion into her face. She sputtered and lost her balance. The knife dropped from her fingers as she sprawled backwards on the table.

"Is she dead?" Lisa asked.

"No," Bram said. "Just sleeping."

Lisa slumped against the counter. "Nathan," she sobbed.

My heart clenched. "It will be okay. We can recombine his ghost with his other half."

"We can?" Her tears slowed.

"Yes." I really, really hoped we could. A lot of people were depending on me to figure this out.

Bram stepped forward. "We have decisions to make. She's a witch, so she won't be charged with a crime when she wakes, but we might be."

Anger boiled up inside of me. "That's wrong."

"Agreed, but there isn't much we can do about it," he said.

Wait a minute. "Did this lunatic split everyone so Violet would sign the divorce papers?"

"Perhaps." Bram opened another bottle of anesthesia potion and poured it in her mouth. "That will make sure she doesn't wake until we want her to. We need to portal her somewhere for safe keeping while we figure this out."

"Let's take her to my house. Lilly will set up a room for her and make sure she doesn't escape."

Bram portaled all three of us back to Lilly much to the surprise of Celia, Dave, and Sadie who were seated in the living room.

"Lilly, please go into lock down and then set up a secure room in the guest bedroom so a witch can't escape," I rattled off.

The lights blinked twice.

"Dave, call the other twins and tell them to be on high alert. We don't know if she was acting alone." I took Lisa's arm and moved her toward the couch. "Sadie can you —?"

Sadie switched into her human form. "Come here, dear. It's all going to be okay." She enveloped Lisa in a hug.

I heard quiet sobbing as I turned and followed Bram. He carried Amber up to the spare bedroom, which Lilly had altered by removing the window. She'd added several locks to the door. Once we had Amber on the bed, I said, "Lilly can you prevent her from using magic?"

The lights blinked once which meant she couldn't.

"She shouldn't wake until I give her the antidote to the anesthesia potion." Bram assured me. We locked her in and then we rejoined Dave, Sadie, Celia, and Lisa on the main floor.

"Now what?" Lisa asked.

"We don't know if she acted alone," I said. "If she did, then she's the only one who can recombine everyone."

Bram frowned. "I wonder if she planned to drain the doubles or came up with that after the mayor changed the law."

"I hate her," Lisa said.

"Do you still have one of the coins?" I asked Bram.

He nodded. "At my house."

"Would you get it for me?"

"How will that help?" Dave asked.

Bram opened a portal, stepped through it and returned a moment later. He held out a clear bowl with the coin inside.

"Come with me." I led him back upstairs and we entered the guest room turned holding cell.

"Dump the coin in her hand."

He did as I asked.

I picked up her limp hand and flipped the coin.

Bram tilted his head. "I think I understand. You're going to make her split into twins."

"That's the plan." I took the bowl from him, scooped the coin off the bedspread and put it in her hand again. We flipped it repeatedly a dozen times.

"Do you think that's enough?" he asked.

"Tomorrow we'll find out."

———— ⌀ ————

CHAPTER 17

The next morning, we all waited to see what would happen.

"If she's split, then she'll have to recombine all the doubles, right?" Lisa asked, like she needed reassurance.

"That is my hope." I drank coffee while I waited for Bram to show up. He'd portaled home to his office to refill his medical bag with supplies.

How long would it be until someone reported Amber missing? She wasn't married, so there wouldn't be a husband searching for her. I doubt Herb actually cared for her. Wait, that was mean of me...even if it was more than likely true.

Since there was nothing else I could do at the moment, I sat at the kitchen table eating donuts, hoping the sugar and fat would sooth my nerves. The vanilla iced cake donut made the world seem like a slightly better place. The cinnamon twist I dunked into my coffee gave me a moment of pure bliss.

Bram portaled into the kitchen. "I think I have everything we need. Have you checked on her?"

"No." I stuck my hand in my pocket and touched the reassuring weight of the Dagger of Life. "I was waiting for back up." And attempting to eat my weight in donuts.

He sighed. "We'll be trusting her to do the right thing."

"So, us not being charged with kidnapping might rely on the morals of a woman who slept with someone else's husband? Great."

We trudged upstairs and opened the door. One Amber sat on the end of the bed looking dazed, while one sat on the floor with her knees pulled up to her chest.

"Can you see her?" the Amber on the bed pointed to the one on the floor.

"Yes," I said. "What do you know about the coins?"

"Keep your mouth shut," Amber on the floor ordered.

"Working with Herb's mother was a stupid idea." Amber on the bed pointed at her other self. "This is all your fault. I was happy selling houses. You became greedy. You took the bait and broke up a marriage."

"If we didn't break them up Mrs. Fairbanks would have found another way," Floor Amber answered. "Now we can have everything we ever wanted: power, money, and respect."

Amber on the bed rubbed her temples. "I highly doubt the respect part of that equation." She sighed and met my gaze. "Hating yourself has taken on a whole new meaning."

"Did you give Violet the game with the coins, so she'd sign the divorce papers?" I asked.

"Yes," Amber on the bed said. "Herb had the papers drawn up six months ago. He was tired of waiting."

"You and Mrs. Fairbanks wore a glamour so no one would recognize you?" I added trying to fill in the blanks.

Amber on the floor laughed. "Mrs. Fairbanks would never set foot in *Tea & Spirits*. That was Herb."

I sucked in a breath. "Seriously? He acted like he didn't know anything about the doubles."

"He's a skilled liar," Amber on the bed said. "If you give me the coin, I can recombine everyone."

"Not before we collect their blood." Floor Amber smacked her palm on the floor for emphasis.

"It's over," I said. "You won't be collecting any more blood."

"Mrs. Fairbanks doesn't take no for an answer," Floor Amber said.

Bram frowned. "How much more blood was she expecting from you?"

"There were two more twins to go: Reed and Lisa."

"What did you do with Nathan's blood?" I asked.

"I sent it through to the bank vault before I went after Lisa." Floor Amber responded. "I like to think ahead."

Her smart alec tone and lack of empathy for my friends made me clench my fists. "So, you're fine with draining two random people who never hurt anyone."

"It's a tough town," Floor Amber said.

"We're not draining my friends." Then I had an idea. I pulled the Dagger of Life from my pocket and flipped it open. "If we drain you, then you'll only be short one person's blood."

"Belinda?" Bram's voice sounded strained.

"You remember what she told Lisa. This won't kill her."

"You wouldn't dare," Floor Lisa said.

"Before coming to Mystic Hills, I wouldn't have considered it. Now it seems only fair that you be subjected to the same fate as your victims."

Bed Amber lunged at me, grabbed the blade, and shoved me aside. I scrambled backwards; certain I would feel the blade drive into my body at any moment. Bed Amber turned and drove the weapon into her twin's neck.

Revulsion rolled over me. My cinnamon twist threatened to come back up.

Floor Amber screamed. Bed Amber chanted something under her breath which kept Floor Amber from breaking free.

I watched as the white handle of the knife turned red. It didn't expand, so the blood must be stored magically inside. I focused on that mystery rather than watching the life drain from Floor Amber's eyes. Five minutes later, Bed Amber, or I suppose just Amber stood. "You have no idea how good that felt." She closed the switch blade, slid the knife in her pocket, and sat back on the bed.

It took me a moment to find my voice. "Can you recombine the twins?"

She nodded. "It's a simple spell reversal. All I need is a coin."

Bram pulled the coin from his pocket, which was now in a clear plastic bag. "Tell me how it works."

"I hold the coin and say, The die is cast. The spell is done. Recombine the halves into one."

"Do it." I took the bag from Bram. "Just know if you're thinking about double crossing us, I am friends with Agatha Fiend."

Amber sucked in a breath.

"No double crosses," I warned.

"No," she assured me.

Agatha was a handy friend to have.

Amber took the coin and dragged it along her palm which produced a drop of blood. "The die is cast. The spell is done. Recombine the halves into one."

Both of her images flickered and then slammed back together like two powerful magnets that had been pulled apart.

"My head," the now singular Amber clutched at her temples.

"Would you like a headache potion?" Bram asked.

Amber blinked and glanced around. "Where am I? How did I get here?"

"You portaled to Bram's office last night," I said. "Don't you remember?" I turned away and whispered, "Lilly, make this room look like a Healer's office."

A wave of neutral color rolled over the room. The walls now appeared gray, and the bed was covered in plain white linens. The other furniture disappeared except for the nightstand which now looked like a metal bedside table.

"What was that?" Amber clutched at the bed sheets.

"What was what?" I pretended the whole room hadn't shifted into something else.

Bram raised his eyebrows at me, but he joined in. "You were quite disoriented when you came in last night."

"What's the last thing you remember?" I asked.

"Herb wanted me to play some game," she said.

"I've heard he's not to be trusted," I said. "Bram can portal you home now if you'd like to sleep in your own bed."

"I don't know what I ever saw in Herb. I can't believe he'd leave me alone when I felt this bad."

"There are definitely more considerate fish in the sea," I said.

"Wait a minute," Amber's eyes narrowed. "We made twins. The game worked."

Oh crap.

She pointed at me. "You. You helped Violet sign the divorce papers, and then Herb wore a glamour and drained the other Violet." She turned to Bram. "I drained Nathan and then you attacked me."

"No," he said. "I used an anesthesia potion to prevent you from injuring someone else."

She squeezed her eyes closed. "That witch, and I mean that both figuratively and literally. Mrs. Fairbanks started all of this. She told me if I didn't drain one of each twin, she'd drain me."

"Sounds like a stellar mother-in-law," I offered.

Amber glared at me and then laughed. "She's terrifying. I had no idea what I was getting into when she asked me to seduce Herb."

Wait. "You went after him?"

"She wanted me to break up their marriage. Anyone could see Violet and Herb weren't happy. I figured I'd be Mrs. Herb Fairbanks for a few years and when I wanted out, I'd hire a younger witch to start the process all over again. It was a business arrangement. I never agreed to drain anyone."

Good to know she had some sort of standards.

"Since you remember what happened, what do you plan to tell Mrs. Fairbanks?" I asked.

Amber sat up straighter. "Stop looking at me like I'm a monster. You do whatever it takes to get ahead in this town. Mrs. Fairbanks is expecting one more person to be drained and the blood to be deposited in her bank account."

"Where are we going to get that many pints of blood?" Bram asked.

I wonder...who would have that much blood and be willing to share it with us. "Celia?" I called out into the hallway.

The tiny sprite buzzed up the stairs and met me in the hallway. I explained the situation with Mrs. Fairbanks. "Can you get Orville to loan you enough blood to make it look like Amber drained one more person?"

"That would be about ten pints," Celia said. "I'm not sure."

"Can you go see him and explain the stakes of this request?"

Celia nodded, opened a portal, and stepped through it.

Bram and Amber were talking, and she didn't look like she planned to attack anyone, so I went downstairs to check on Lisa.

She sat on the couch with her head in her hands.

I sat next to her. "How are you doing?"

She glanced up at me. "I had the weirdest dream about curling my hair and dating Nathan." One of her curls slid in front of her face. She grabbed it and her eyes went huge. "Oh my gosh. It was real? I mean Nathan? That was real, too?"

"His ghost came to me after he was drained, and the first thing he said was, 'Save Lisa.'"

"Really?" Her eyes filled with hope.

I nodded.

Lisa's phone rang. "Excuse me." She answered it. "Hello, Nathan? Yes. I'm fine. Yes. I remember. I'm at Belinda's house. Do you want to come pick me up?"

Her face colored as she ended the call. "We're going out for breakfast."

"Good for you."

My phone rang and my heart skipped a beat. Was Reed calling me? "Hello?"

"Belinda, it's Mrs. Kingsley. Both Violet and I have recombined. Thanks for whatever you did."

I pushed aside the disappointment that Reed didn't reach out to me and focused on the issue at hand. Should I tell Mrs. Kingsley about Herb draining the other Violet? It wouldn't change anything. Still I felt the need to warn her. "I'm glad to hear you're both back to normal. Make sure Violet doesn't spend any time alone with Herb or accept any expensive looking flowers from a stranger."

"I don't think that will be a problem." Mrs. Kingsley paused. "Just so I understand, are you saying he was responsible for the flowers and what followed?"

"Yes."

"Thank you for sharing that disturbing information. It may come in useful if Violet ever has second thoughts about that miserable excuse for a man." She hung up.

The house phone rang. Before I could stand and walk into the kitchen, Victor answered. I heard him say Reed's name. He laughed and then called out, "Belinda, Reed is back to one person."

"Good."

A tiny portal appeared above the living room fireplace. Celia flew through it and buzzed up the stairs. I jogged after her and followed her into the spare bedroom where Amber sat on the bed. Bram stood leaning against the wall.

Now the size of a barbie, Celia landed on the dresser and held a contract which she read out loud.

"I the undersigned promise not to seek retribution against any friend of Celia's, which includes any friend of Belinda Harbinger in exchange for ten pints of blood being transferred to the account of my choosing." Celia held it out to Amber. "Sign it."

"I'd like to read it first." Amber snatched the paper from the sprite's grip and read it before holding out her hand. "A pen, please."

Bram pulled one from his pocket.

She signed and handed Celia the document. "Tell him to send the blood to my account. I'll transfer it to Mrs. Fairbanks, so she knows it came from me. I'll make sure to tell her I reversed the spell once I had the last of the blood." She handed the pen back to Bram and then opened a portal and stepped through.

"It's done?" I asked, hoping I was right.

"It should be." Bram turned and walked from the room. "I need a cup of tea."

I followed him down the stairs and into the kitchen. A pot of tea and a plate of scones and cinnamon rolls sat on the kitchen table.

Bram paused and pointed at the tea, "Lilly did you do this?"

The lights blinked twice.

"Thank you." He sat and poured himself a cup. I joined him at the table, feeling slightly defeated.

Celia flew in and sat cross-legged on the table. "Belinda, you fixed everything. Why don't you seem happier?"

It was hard to explain. "I helped with a problem, but I didn't really fix anything. Mrs. Fairbanks and all the other witches still control everything and can pretty much do whatever they want without repercussions. That's wrong."

"That's Mystic Hills," Bram said.

I sipped my newly poured cup of tea. "It doesn't have to be this way."

A knock on the back door made me jump. Before I could stand to answer it, Lisa ran in and flung the door open.

Nathan entered the room, wrapped his arms around Lisa and pressed his mouth against hers.

I fought the urge to sigh at the movie-worthy scene.

The kiss ended, and Nathan said, "When Amber came at me, all I could think about was trying to protect you. I'm sorry I didn't do a better job."

Lisa sniffled. "She snuck up on both of us. I'm sorry I couldn't stop her from draining you." She turned to me. "Do we need to be afraid of her?"

"No." I gave a quick summary of Celia's contract with Amber.

"That was smart," Nathan said.

"Can we go to breakfast?" Lisa asked.

In response, Nathan opened the back door and they left.

Before the door even closed Reed came in smiling. "Good morning, everyone."

"Morning," I forced a cheery tone.

He joined us at the table. "You'll be glad to know Angry Reed has left the building. After seeing myself in that unflattering light, I've decided to let go of the past." He placed a warm hand on my forearm. "I consider you a friend."

The genuine smile on his face and the heat of his touch had me tearing up. "Thank you. That means a lot."

"Is my dad around?" he asked.

"I'm in the living room," Victor called out.

Reed grabbed a cinnamon roll before heading in to see his father.

I wiped at the tears I hadn't been able to hold back, and realized Bram was studying me. "Sorry. It's been a stressful couple of days, and I never thought Reed would forgive me."

"And you want to be his friend?" His tone implied he was asking something else, something more substantial.

How should I respond? "Having Reed hate me was painful. Like him, I'm ready to leave the past behind and move forward with my life."

He took a bite of his scone and stared at the wall. After a sip of tea he said, "If I asked you on a real date, would you say yes?"

"Hedging your bets?" I asked.

He grinned. "Something like that."

"You'll be relieved to know I would say yes."

"Good." He took another sip of his tea.

I waited. He didn't say anything.

"Any time now," I muttered as I buttered a scone.

"Now you're being pushy," he teased.

I pointed at him with the butter knife which was still in my hand. "I am armed."

He held his hands up like he was surrendering. "May I take you out to dinner Saturday?"

"Yes," I said.

Reed walked back through the kitchen. "Took you long enough, Bram." He grabbed another cinnamon roll and headed for the door. "Jezelle was going to dose you with a courage potion if you didn't make a move soon."

Bram didn't blink. "Tell my cousin to behave because it would be a shame if I accidentally switched her birth control potion for a fertility potion."

"What?" Reed's eyes went huge, and his face turned red.

Bram pointed at him. "Remember who you're messing with."

"That's just evil." Reed left by the back door.

Bram glanced at me. "I'd never do that, but I wanted to take him down a notch."

"He deserved it."

We sat in comfortable silence, and then I remembered I'd never shared Agatha's story with him. Was now the time?

I glanced at him.

"What?" he asked. "Are you reconsidering our date?"

"No. I have some totally off topic information I planned to share with you at some point, but it's kind of sad."

He reached up and rubbed his eyes. "Do I need to hear it at this moment, because after the last couple of days I could use a break from drama."

"Then I'll tell you another time."

"It's nothing vital I should know?" he asked.

"Not at all. It's a new spin on something that happened a long time ago. It can wait."

"Good." He finished his tea and set the cup on the saucer. "I'm going home to take a nap." He placed his hand on top of mine. "I'll pick you up Saturday at six."

"Sounds good."

Bram opened a portal and left. Happiness flowed through me. I did a small celebratory dance in my chair. I had a date with Bram. I was moving on with my life.

Later that night, I went upstairs and pulled out my journals. I ran my fingers over the embossed sunflowers, but picked up the one with Memories written on the front in gold script. After breaking the spine, I stared at the page. Where to start?

Should I write about the coins and how we solved the problem? I felt like it was a job well done. Even though several of my friends had been drained, no one died. Me being able to see ghosts actually saved lives, so maybe it wasn't such a terrible gift. And the older man named Thomas, well I still didn't understand what happened to him. Since he'd been counting down the days til he could see his wife again, his death didn't seem tragic, and I was happy to leave that mystery to the police.

Reed forgave me for not coming back to him. Part of me had hoped he might want to be more than friends, but I really liked Jezelle, and Bram's smile made my heart beat faster. It was time for me to let go of the past and move on to make new memories.

It helped to realize Agatha and her vengeance hexes might keep the evil witches in check. Knowing there was someone out there who could send karmic retribution your way should deter some bad behavior. It was time to focus on the positive side of Mystic Hills.

First on the list: I had friends and found family in Mystic Hills. Seeing ghosts wasn't terrible. Reed had forgiven me. Bram asked me on a date.

Despite the random mayhem, I could see a real future for myself in Mystic Hills.

TEASER
Spellbound In Mystic Hills
Mysteries of Mystic Hills Book 3

Friday night, a gray form whooshed into my room interrupting my reading time. The swirling mass solidified into a woman.

"What is going on?" she yelled.

"Mrs. Fairbanks?"

The ghost focused on me. "What did you do?"

What did I do? "Nothing. I think you died."

"Dead? I can't be dead." She poofed out of existence.

Had Mrs. Fairbank's evil ways finally caught up with her? Who knew? Time for me to play my part. I grabbed my phone but before I could call Reed, it rang.

"Hello?"

"Belinda, this is Violet. Don't worry if any annoying mother and son ghosts show up. Agatha is draining them to the point of death and then reviving them."

"Oh," was all I managed to say. Goosebumps pebbled my arms. It's not like I could cast stones, I'd been ready to use the Dagger of Life to drain Amber.

"As karma goes, it's mild retribution according to Agatha, but once she heard the whole story about how my mother-in-law blamed me for being barren while she dosed her son with an infertility potion, she was more than happy to help."

"Okay." They'd gone to Agatha for a vengeance hex. I hadn't seen that coming.

"Herb's ghost will probably stop by next."

"And then Amber?" I asked.

"No. Her personal hell has just begun. I'm leaving her to it."

"Okay then. I'll ignore the ghosts."

"Tell me you understand why we're doing this," Violet's tone wavered.

"I understand." And I did. They were only doing to Mrs. Fairbanks and Herb what they had done to Violet and her mother. There was one problem. "Won't they turn you into the police?"

"No. Agatha will make sure they don't." She ended the call.

I picked up my book and opened it. A few pages later, Herb's ghost popped into existence at the foot of my bed.

"Hello," he yelled. "Can you hear me?"

I pretended I couldn't hear him because he didn't deserve any comfort at the moment. He'd figure out soon enough what was going on.

He spun in a circle. "Hello, can anyone help—" Poof, he disappeared.

"Good riddance," I snuggled into my bed and focused on my book.

Half an hour before Bram was due to pick me up Saturday night for our first official date, the house was ghost free. I didn't mind helping those who had died move on, but sometimes the whole I see dead people thing got in the way of a my regularly scheduled life.

I checked the mirror one more time before heading downstairs to wait in the kitchen. My chestnut hair was pulled back in a low bun, and my gauzy summer dress did a good job skimming my curves without showing off too much. Time to stop fussing and focus on having fun.

Downstairs, I found Sadie sitting on the kitchen table in cat form, while Dave sat in one of the chairs drinking a cup of tea.

"Don't you look lovely," Dave said as a way of greeting.

"Thank you."

"Where is Bram taking you for dinner?" Sadie asked.

"I'm not sure." I poured myself a cup of tea and joined them at the table. We made small talk as the clock ticked down. When it hit five after six, a hollow feeling invaded my stomach.

"What time is he picking you up?" Dave asked.

"Six," I said.

"He is a Healer," Sadie said. "Maybe he's with a patient."

"That's probably it." If that were true, he could have texted to say he was running late. I checked my phone. No text. No message. No missed phone call. Okay. Not a big deal.

At quarter after six, a car came down the driveway. I didn't jump up because I recognized the rumble of that Mustang. It was Reed.

"Don't say anything to him about this," I said.

The back door opened, and Reed came in. He was all fair skin and dark hair and deep brown soulful eyes and even though I was dating, or let me rephrase that, even though I thought I was dating Bram, my heart skipped a beat.

"Hello." His gaze fixed on me, not in a lustful way, more like a confused way. "I thought you had a date with Bram."

"I do," and that came out defensive.

"He's running a little late," Dave said.

I resisted the urge to kick my friend under the table.

"I'm sure he'll be here soon." Reed walked into the living room and headed upstairs to see his father.

The clock hit six-thirty and my stomach growled. "This is ridiculous." I hadn't eaten much today because I was nervous about the date, which was funny now that the date didn't seem to be happening.

"You could call him," Sadie suggested.

"I'll give him fifteen more minutes."

At six forty five Reed and Victor came down the stairs. Victor paused and opened his mouth.

"Don't say it," I warned.

"I'm sure—" Reed joined in.

"Go." I pointed at the back door.

At seven I checked my phone one more time. The blank screen mocked me. This wasn't a big deal. He was probably treating someone. "Should I call him?"

"Yes," Sadie said. "Bram is polite to a fault. There has to be a good reason he stood—that he's late."

I wanted to believe that. This was my first date since breaking things off with my ex. I was supposed to be moving on with my life. Dang it.

I flipped my phone open and dialed his number.

"Hello?" Bram sounded normal.

"It's Belinda."

"Yes." That was it. No sorry I'm late. No excuse about having an emergency. Nothing. I'd expected something completely different and now I had no idea how to respond.

"Belinda, did you need something?"

My stomach felt like it dropped to my shoes while my brain spun. He had asked me on a date. Right? We'd sat at this table, and he'd asked me to dinner. Unless I was nuts. Which seemed more possible by the minute.

"If you're not injured, I need to let you go," he said. "It's been a long day."

"Goodbye." I hung up and stared at my phone. A cold pit of insecurity opened in my gut. Wait. I was a grown woman. A man changing his mind about me shouldn't make me feel this vulnerable.

"What did he say?" Sadie asked.

"Nothing." My eyes heated and I blinked back tears of frustration. "It's like he had no idea why I'd called him." Or the more painful interpretation...I was not a person of interest. What the heck? Had he forgotten? How was that possible? "Did I imagine him asking me on a date?"

"No," Sadie said. "Superior Familiar hearing. I heard him ask you. Plus Reed teased him about it."

Okay. So, it had happened but since then he decided he wasn't interested. "I don't understand." I would not cry over a missed dinner date. "Even though I'm confused, I do know one thing: I want pie. Who wants to go to Chanda's with me?"

Sadie shifted into her human form wearing an orange maxi-dress. Her blond bob was held back on one side with a decorative gold barrette. "I'm in."

Dave paused. "Whatever you two want. I'm happy to join or I could stay home, put my feet up, and read a book."

"Come with us," I said. "I don't want this to turn into a gripe session. I want to eat good food and share good conversation." And maybe forget this whole Bram fiasco ever happened.

Traffic on the way to Chanda's seemed unusually light. I parked right in front of the restaurant. Once we were seated, the waitress brought a basket of bread and a pitcher of ice water to our table. "This is to tide you over. Several servers and a chef skipped out on us tonight. We're calling in replacements, but service may be a bit slow til everyone arrives."

"That's odd," Dave said.

I buttered a piece of bread still warm from the oven and took a bite. It was heavenly. "I don't care about dating. I just want this bread."

The waiter arrived. "What can I get for you this evening?"

"I want peach pie with ice cream and then the house salad with grilled chicken."

The young man blinked. "That's reverse of the normal order."

"I'm aware," I told him.

"All right." He took my friends' orders, and we kept the conversation light. An hour later, with my stomach full, I felt like the world was a much brighter place... until Bram walked in with another woman. And not just any woman, she was a bronze skinned female fairy who moved with a grace I'd never possess. Heads turned at her little black dress which left nothing to the imagination.

I gripped my fork tight enough to bend it while I focused on breathing in and out and not screaming. The not screaming part was the hardest. I wanted to march over there and demand answers...like why in the heck had he stood me up to go out with another woman? Why not man up and tell me he'd changed his mind?

"Well that's... freaking rude," Sadie said.

Dave leaned closer to Sadie. "You are one of the most beautiful women I've ever seen. I know you're Belinda's friend, but I can't for the life of me remember your name."

Sadie froze for a second and then said, "Sadie."

"It's lovely to meet you, Sadie."

What. The. Heck.

I scanned the room. Two women at the table next to us seemed baffled. I walked over and joined them. "Excuse me. Did you notice anything strange tonight?"

The blond nodded. "My date left to use the restroom, and he never came back. I don't know where he went."

The other woman said, "My husband never showed. I called him. He acted like he didn't even recognize me."

All over the dining room the men seemed confused or irritated, and the women appeared panicked.

I returned to my table. "The males all seem to be under a spell."

Dave chuckled. "Good one." He pointed behind me. "Here come's someone who is definitely under your spell."

I glanced over my shoulder. Reed strode toward me with an easy manner, like he knew exactly what he was doing. Thank goodness. Maybe this spell hadn't affected everyone.

He sat in the chair next to me. "Here you are. I've been looking all over for you."

"Really? Why?"

Instead of answering, he leaned toward me. I thought he was going to whisper something but then he pressed his mouth against mine. The contact was brief, but warmth flowed through my body. My brain screamed it was wrong, but my heart and my hormones had other ideas.

He pulled away and said, "Don't sound so surprised. Can't a guy miss his girlfriend?"

Girlfriend? Uh-oh.

I hope you enjoyed Belinda's latest adventure. Want to find out why the men of Mystic Hills are having memory problems? Check out the next book in the series, Spellbound in Mystic Hills coming soon.

If you enjoyed the read, please consider leaving a review on your preferred retail site. Reviews really do help sell books and I would greatly appreciate it.

Sincerely,

Chris Cannon

Don't miss out!

Visit the website below and you can sign up to receive emails whenever Chris Cannon publishes a new book. There's no charge and no obligation.

https://books2read.com/r/B-A-EDWG-EIALC

BOOKS 2 READ

Connecting independent readers to independent writers.

About the Author

Chris Cannon lives in Southern Illinois with her husband and various furry beasts. She believes coffee is the Elixir of Life. Most evenings after work you can find her sipping caffeine and writing paranormal cozy mysteries.

Read more at https://www.chriscannonauthor.com/.

Milton Keynes UK
Ingram Content Group UK Ltd.
UKHW011817190923
428965UK00001BI/204

9 798987 869857